Island Interlude

G·K Hall &Co.

***Also by Jane Edwards
in Large Print:***

Dangerous Odyssey
The Ghost of Castle Kilgarrom
The Hesitant Heart
The Houseboat Mystery
Susannah Is Missing!
Tangled Heritage
Terror by Design
What Happened to Amy?
Yellow Ribbons

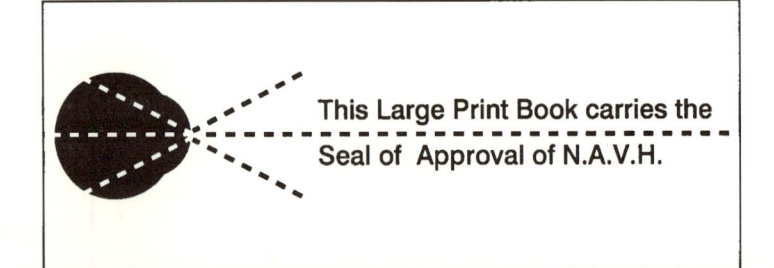

This Large Print Book carries the
Seal of Approval of N.A.V.H.

Island Interlude

Jane Edwards

G.K. Hall & Co. • Thorndike, Maine

© Copyright, 1969, by Jane Edwards

All rights reserved.

Published in 2000 by arrangement with Jane Edwards

G.K. Hall Large Print Paperback Series.

The text of this Large Print edition is unabridged.
Other aspects of the book may vary from the original edition.

Set in 16 pt. Plantin.

Printed in the United States on permanent paper.

Library of Congress Cataloging-in-Publication Data

Edwards, Jane (Jane Campbell), 1932–
   Island interlude / Jane Edwards.
      p. cm.
   ISBN 0-7838-9131-8 (lg. print : sc : alk. paper)
   1. Large type books. I. Title.
PS3555.D933 I85   2000
  813'.54—dc21   00-033495

For a delightful aunt and uncle,
JANE and JOE DREWICKE

Chapter One

Midway down the airliner's ramp a shimmering wave of heat engulfed her. It bubbled moistly up from the hard-packed earth of the runway, a mute but eloquent testimony to the half-continent she had spanned since dawn. Replacing the crisp Bay breezes she had left behind was a limp, gauzy curtain of air, almost tangibly alive with the cloying, sticky-sweet perfume of oleander.

She was, thought Denise O'Shea, an awfully long way from home.

The line moved slowly. A few of her fellow passengers lagged behind, casting wistful glances at the emptying jet. The abrupt change in climate *was* rather dismaying. But wistfulness, Denise had learned, was generally futile — and invariably time-consuming. Foolish in this case, too, since the terminal building was undoubtedly air-conditioned. Outside, the temperature seemed to have achieved astronomical proportions.

Heads turned to stare in admiration as the tall, slim girl walked with supple grace across the apron of the field. Sunlight sparked an answering glint from the raven-black hair which curved smoothly about her head in a becoming cap. In contrast, her complexion was startlingly fair, and beneath ebony brows her eyes were a deep, vibrant blue.

Denise stepped inside the waiting room, welcoming the rush of refrigerated air against her face. For a moment she paused at the wall of glass overlooking the field. A trolley rumbled by, and she watched as her trio of suitcases was transferred from the jet's cavernous hold to the baggage compartment of a smaller aircraft. Then, secure in the knowledge that she and her wardrobe were still traveling companions, she turned toward the reservations desk.

Noon appeared to be a popular time of day, both for flights arriving in New Orleans and those which were departing. A bevy of tourists flocked around the ticket counters. Caught up in the throng, Denise inched ahead. Voices, some brisk and Northern, others a langorous Dixie drawl, eddied in circles around her.

"— fascinating as that swampy bayou country?"

"Sixty thousand dollars worth of diamonds. Imagine being hoodwinked . . ."

"— thought we were on Bourbon Street, but his old Creole woman . . ."

"Nothing but tourists in the French Quarter. I told Agnes . . ."

"— didn't even know it had been stolen until she dropped the necklace!"

"— heavenly doughnuts. I must have gained five pounds."

"Flight 607 to Cartuga." Denise's turn had arrived. She pushed her ticket folder across the counter. "Will it depart on time?"

The reservationist smiled reassuringly, validated the ticket stub and passed it back. "Exactly on schedule. Take-off at 12:52. Enjoy your trip, Miss O'Shea."

After freshening her make-up in the ladies' lounge, Denise skirted the crowded waiting room and paused at the entrance to the coffee shop. To her disappointment, not only was every table occupied, but impatient travelers stood three-deep around the counter.

From a table nearby a gay voice pulled her back as she started to turn away. "Hi," called a petite blonde girl, with short curly hair and an enviable tan. "Would you like to sit over here?"

"Love to." Smiling her thanks, Denise quickly accepted the invitation. She reached for the menu to avoid staring at her table-mate. The girl's face was tantalizingly familiar.

"I'm delighted that you arrived in time to connect with the flight I'm taking," the blonde girl declared. "We can sit together on the plane. And won't it be fun —" She broke off, a flush of sudden embarrassment staining her cheeks. "You *are* Denise O'Shea, aren't you? The swimmer?"

"Why, yes. How —"

"Unfair advantage, really. I had been keeping a look-out for you, hoping your departure for

Cartuga would coincide with mine. I'm Natalie Engstromm."

Denise's perplexed expression cleared. "Tennis! Oh, my goodness, no wonder I felt so certain we had met before. I must have seen your picture in the paper dozens of times!"

"No more often than I've seen yours." Natalie dimpled. "Every press photographer in the country flipped his flashbulbs when you won that gold medal in the Olympic games last summer."

She paused while a waitress took their orders for iced coffee, then continued on in the same enthusiastic tone. "To think that after wanting to meet you for years, I'll actually be working with you! My Aunt Florence is an old friend of Martin Lorrimer. When I accepted the tennis pro job at his new hotel, he wrote her a personal letter saying he considered himself extremely fortunate to have hired both of us. You to keep an eye on his Olympic-sized pool, and me to handle the racquet racket."

She sipped the cold beverage, muffling a giggle. "How the poor man will lose face, should somebody drown or break a leg leaping over the net!"

For the first time in weeks Denise found herself laughing wholeheartedly. This dainty, demure-looking girl who had won top tennis honors for America on several occasions possessed a sense of humor to match her well-deserved reputation in the world of sports.

"Have you any idea of what the Hotel Caribe Azure will be like?" Denise asked eagerly. "My only contact with Mr. Lorrimer has been my mail."

"Mine too," Natalie admitted. "But from the advance publicity I understand the place is absolutely fabulous. It is built right on the ocean front a couple of miles from San Marco, the capital city. In my aunt's opinion, only the poverty of her people prevents Cartuga from becoming famous as one of the Caribbean's true beauty spots."

Within a short time a warm friendship had sprung up between the girls. Denise, a Californian, learned that Natalie's home town was Baltimore, Maryland. Although both young athletes had traveled extensively, this was the first visit for both to either New Orleans or the island which was to be their home for the next year.

A loudspeaker announcement heralded the departure of flight 607. Following a stream of other Southbound travelers, the girls took adjacent seats aboard the airliner. Despite the fact that the Caribbean's main tourist season was not due to begin until December, still two months away, the plane carried a full pay-load. Denise wondered if the opening of Martin Lorrimer's new hotel had drawn all these visitors to Cartuga.

Shortly after take-off Natalie nudged Denise, and lowered her voice. "Look," she said conspiratorially. "There's Luana de Cortez. Four rows up, on the right."

"Surrounded by an entourage of admiring males, just like in her latest movie," Denise observed. "Isn't she beautiful! Do you suppose she is headed for the Hotel Caribe Azure, too?"

"I'm certain that if she is, we will soon read about it. Most of those 'admiring males' are journalists," laughed Natalie, who had glimpsed a number of press cameras being stowed away when the group came aboard. "Travel columnists for the major newspapers and magazines, I'll warrant. What a life — being paid to visit one luxurious resort after another so that the reading public can be kept up-to-date on vacation spots!"

Denise smiled. "I doubt that we will be exactly overworked ourselves. Not everyone would consider it back-breaking labor to splash around in a pool or lob balls across a net all day. Although," she added more soberly, "some people may be curious to know why we both dropped our amateur standings to accept these jobs."

"I guess I just got tired of being a glory hound." Natalie's pretty face twisted in a distasteful grimace. "That's what a fellow I once knew called me. And after five or six years of continuous competition you *do* begin to wonder whether life might not have more to offer than blue ribbons and loving cups."

"You too? Exactly the same thought occurred to me," Denise fervently agreed. "Especially during those rigorous training programs which discourage practically all social activity."

Her lips tightened. "While I was faithfully going to bed at nine o'clock every night, a cute little redhead walked off with my fiance. She was a swimmer, too — an Aquacade star. It didn't take her long to convince Tim that the salary paid professional performers could be very attractive. For months he had slaved to win a spot on the water sports team, only to walk out at the last minute. Two weeks before our crew was ready to leave for the Games, he joined the Aquacade troupe. Told the coach he saw no future in competing for a piece of 'display jewelry.' "

Denise stared sightlessly out of the plane's window. Angry tears smarted at the corners of her eyes. She blinked them back, but there was no denying that Tim's defection still hurt. The ridge grooved on her finger by his engagement ring had vanished without a trace; that had smoothed out soon after she had boxed the tiny diamond and returned it to him by mail. The jagged rip in her self-esteem was healing more slowly. An occasional poignant memory still had the power to wrench that half-closed scar.

"He married the redhead a week later," she concluded the bitter tale. "Possibly he had the right idea, after all. Former Olympics competitors don't rate a pension."

"No, nothing that tangible," Natalie quietly agreed.

The significance of this remark was not lost on

Denise. True, she acknowledged, aside from the medal there was no overt reward. Just a blaze of proud patriotism. A glow, still awesome in retrospect, when *The Star Spangled Banner* rang out over a hushed assemblage and that splendid red, white and blue pennant billowed victoriously from the flagpole soaring above the winner's circle.

Payment in full!

She smiled an apology to Natalie. "Heavens, I don't know what came over me. It isn't often that I get to feeling so sorry for myself. Hope I didn't sprinkle your shoulder too liberally with my maudlin tears."

"Well, you might have tested the fabric to make sure it was drip-dry!" the blonde girl retorted — and they both laughed.

A delicious luncheon was served while they were aloft. Unfortunately, their enjoyment of the meal was marred by Luana de Cortez's childish behavior. The tempestuous Latin star flared into a series of noisy antics calculated to grip the attention of every man aboard.

Wavering between amusement and annoyance, Denise noted that the technique seemed highly effective. The lone hold-out was a rugged, broad-shouldered man of about thirty, dressed in casual but well-tailored clothes. He appeared to be quite impervious to the actress's charms. In fact, after an especially loud outburst, he cast the glamor queen a glare of vehement dislike.

Then his shoulders tilted in a disgusted shrug before his gaze reverted to the paper-bound book in his lap.

Something faintly reminiscent about that gesture piqued Denise's curiosity. Another celebrity? Not, she decided, a movie star. *Somebody*, though. That stalwart physique and the shock of red-brown hair were vaguely familiar. But his name, if she had ever known it, had settled to the deepest recesses of her memory. No amount of persuasive cogitation could dredge it out. Since the matter was of only passing interest, she soon stopped prodding her unresponsive powers of recollection.

The airliner slackened speed and began to lose altitude. Gradually, almost imperceptibly, its nose dipped seaward. Descending from the misty heights, its passengers were treated to the sight of a verdant chain of islands, strung out like a handful of scattered jewels to ornament the translucent waters of the Caribbean.

Denise caught her breath. "Talk about million dollar views! Why hasn't some enterprising realtor thought of renting out cloud space up here?" She flattened her nose against the glass. "How clear the water is! Keep a lookout for sunken pirate ships, Nat. Some of them were lost in less than thirty feet of water. I'm sure it must be possible to see down that far on a day like today!"

Natalie's tan curdled to a pistachio green. She jerked back from the spectacular panorama,

"The thought of all that water simply terrifies me," she confessed. "I — I never learned to swim."

Minutes later the plane glided low over an island whose windward side was steeply mountainous. Every aspect of the terrain fascinated Denise — the shacks clinging perilously to the sides of cliffs, the occasional sugar cane fields wherever the land was flat enough for cultivation — and finally a jumbled vista of San Marco itself.

Somewhere down there lay her destiny. What would the coming year bring? Adventure? Romance? Happiness? In a way, she preferred not knowing. Life's surprises were usually worth waiting for.

"You can open your eyes now," she prodded Natalie. "We're coming in to Cartuga!"

Chapter Two

The Customs inspection was a mere formality. The tiny island democracy required only proof of citizenship and a declaration of valuables carried before extending a hospitable welcome to all visitors from the United States. But the representatives of even the friendliest countries are usually impersonal, and Denise gained the impression that behind their warm reception lay the solid influence of Martin Lorrimer. The words "Hotel Caribe Azure" might have been a magical incantation, so speedily did they call forth cordial attention from the Cartugan officials. Uniformed inspectors chalked the girls' suitcases without so much as a glance inside.

This deferential treatment did not escape Denise's notice. Her eagerness to meet her employer burgeoned.

Natalie, however, voiced a complaint. "I suppose that vote of confidence was a tribute to our sweet, honest faces, but really! We could have been smuggling in crates of contraband, for all they knew!"

"Who, us?" Denise laughed. "I suspect that any smuggling which takes place is routed in the opposite direction. Into the States, not away from it."

With unconcealed interest she gazed around at the low, whitewashed buildings comprising the airport. Equipment seemed adequate, if strictly utilitarian, and while construction was complete, the almost total absence of costly extras such as landscaping gave the sprawling field a raw, new-born appearance. Remembering Natalie's earlier remark about the poverty of these islanders, Denise reflected that the lack of "frills" was most likely part of a national austerity program.

"It looks to me as if most Cartugans must struggle to supply their families with the bare necessities of life," she added. "Anyone who slipped illicit baggage past the Customs inspectors in hopes of finding a wealthy buyer here would be taking quite a chance."

Natalie nodded. "Guess you're right. The New Orleans paper this morning carried a front-page spread about a clever jewel robbery which took place there. Probably it was that article which made me think of contraband. If I were the thief, I wouldn't be lingering in Louisiana with sixty thousand dollars worth of diamonds in my pocket!"

"And you think Cartuga would serve as a good hide-out?" Denise teased. "In that case we will have to be extra careful when striking up acquaintances!"

Come to think of it, she recalled, tucking her overnight bag under her arm, she had heard snatches of conversation regarding a jewel robbery. Two shrill-voiced women had been discussing it while standing in line at the airport ticket counter. Something . . . something about a necklace being dropped.

She straightened up, mentally casting the topic aside. Her major concern at the moment centered around arranging transportation to the hotel.

Denise and Natalie had been among the first to leave the plane, and their speedy by-pass of Customs' red-tape had given them an even greater lead on their fellow passengers. A few other travelers were just beginning to trickle through the barrier to the rear of the terminal when a swarm of youths popped like jacks-in-a-box from a nearby building and descended upon the girls with raucous, insistent offers of service.

"Carry your bags, Senorita?"

"A guide, pretty ladies, to show you the sights of our most beautiful city?"

"The finest taxicab in all of San Marco —"

Natalie clung with determination to her luggage, which seemed to be in imminent danger of being carried off in three different directions. Nor had Denise's protestations in slow but well-accented Spanish any effect on the boys. There was something almost frightening in the persistent way each of the lads demanded that he alone be chosen for the job.

"*Un momento, por favor!*" she pleaded again.

Scarcely able to make herself heard, she cast a harried backwards glance at the Customs barrier. To her great relief she caught sight of the tall, broad-shouldered man who had been seated several rows ahead of them on the plane.

He strode into the center of the group. *"Muchachos!"*

That lone authoritative word captured their attention. He clapped one boy on the shoulder, pointed to a second youth, and dispersed the others with a few rapid-fire phrases which diverted the clamorous stream of humanity in the direction of the tourists who were just emerging from the immigration shed.

"A whole battalion of Marines couldn't have come to our rescue more effectively," Denise thanked him.

Natalie, too, expressed her admiration. "How on earth did you persuade them to leave? They wouldn't even *listen* to us!"

"Of course they wouldn't," the man chuckled. "In Cartuga it's open season on tourists the year 'round!"

"Did I hear you say *'muy rico'* — very rich?" Denise puzzled, having comprehended no more than half of his auctioneer-type monologue.

A look of mischief flared briefly in his eyes. "I believe I did happen to mention that a certain well-known film star was also a passenger aboard flight number 607," he admitted. "Our young friends couldn't pass up an opportunity like that. Everyone knows that famous actresses earn a great many pesos."

Grinning good-naturedly, he directed the two

boys who remained to transfer the luggage to a curbside area at the front of the terminal. He himself shouldered a worn golf bag, slinging the heavy case to his back with the ease of long practice. Sympathy touched his face as he watched the youths stagger manfully ahead with their burdens.

"Don't think too harshly of these kids. It's their only way of earning a living, and that lean and hungry look isn't a sham."

"No," Denise contritely agreed. "I don't suppose it is."

Metal clubs clicked dully together as the golf bag was twitched farther back over his shoulder. As if a dial had been suddenly turned, Denise's memory responded. Her mind conjured up a long-forgotten image of her father seated before the television set. His favorite program, *Golf Circuit, U.S.A.*, was in progress, and —

"Weren't you going to introduce yourself, Mr. Gates?" she asked.

His eyes, clear and steady under the red-brown hair and brows, looked momentarily startled. "How very nice of you to remember," he said quietly.

"Shouldn't I have?"

"It's been more than two years . . . nearly all of my gallery deserted to more active golfers when an injury pulled me out of the game."

Again her gaze swung to the jingling bag of clubs. "But now you've started to play again? My Dad will be delighted. He's an incurable golf buff. Not championship caliber like yourself, but good."

With a rueful laugh Roger Gates denied that he meant to challenge Tiger Woods for top honors just yet. "I'm still coddling along a couple of ailing vertebrae," he explained. "In order to earn eating money while they heal, I've taken a job as golf pro at the new Caribe Azure here in Cartuga. Perhaps you've heard of the hotel?"

Denise and Natalie burst out laughing. They quickly relieved his bewilderment by mentioning their own names and declaring that they had been hired in similar capacities.

One of the red-brown brows shot skyward. He inclined his head in a slight bow, murmuring an impudent comment about the "distinguished company" in which he found himself.

"Nothing but the best for Martin Lorrimer, eh? Must be great to have lucre enough to indulge one's every whim."

Denise took umbrage at his tone of voice. "Possibly Mr. Lorrimer prefers to have nothing but the best for the guests of his hotel," she coolly suggested. "Besides, hiring us is really a very sound business practice. With well-known personalities in charge of the sports program, the Caribe Azure can expect to draw a high percentage of the athletically-minded vacationers who visit this part of the Caribbean."

"I stand corrected." Roger Gates made no effort to conceal his amusement.

Natalie, anxious to restore peace between her companions, quickly pointed to a gleaming new station wagon which had glided to the curb.

"The welcoming committee," she announced. "Or is it? Dear me, doesn't he look flustered?"

Alighting from the car with the assistance of the driver was a rather portly gentleman of early middle age. His white suit appeared to be a half-size too snug, but even the starchy collar binding his neck seemed hardly enough to account for his all too evident discomfiture.

"Senorita Engstromm? Senorita O'Shea? Senor Gates? It is a pleasure, an honor, to greet such distinguished persons. I am Leon Perdigo, manager of the Hotel Caribe Azure. On behalf of Senor Lorrimer, I am most gratified to welcome you to Cartuga."

The speech continued for some minutes longer. Denise maintained a polite listening stance while struggling to unravel the flowery phrases of Castile from the clipped British accent with which they were delivered. She lost the thread entirely when a touring car of ancient vintage wheezed to a halt behind the station wagon.

Perdigo's plump hands twisted in distress.

"Lamentably, the second fine automobile provided by the hotel for the transportation of its guests has been stricken by some mysterious malaise." Perspiration glistened across his brow. "This unfortunate state of affairs was naturally not anticipated by Senor Lorrimer when he instructed me to escort the three so-famous athletes as well as the beauteous Senorita de Cortez to the hotel. I am desolated that insufficient space..."

"What you mean is that you want us to ride in that old rattletrap so Luscious Luana and her ink-stained retinue can zoom up to the Caribe Azure in air-conditioned, V-8 comfort," Roger Gates breezily interrupted. "Sure, why not? I'm game. Unless, of course, my illustrious companions insist upon a more elegant mode of transportation."

His side-long glance at Denise dared her to fan the argument. To evade the challenge would be cowardly, yet his mocking manner of speech had already goaded her into making one heated retort. Denise decided that unless she intended to spend the next twelve months in verbal combat with a fellow worker, she had better make it clear immediately that his sardonic jibes bothered her not in the least.

"It is we who should be desolate, tearing you away from the hotel at such a busy time," she assured Senor Perdigo. "This automobile appears to be quite substantial. And, of course, we are most fortunate in having Mr. Gates along to tend to our luggage. I trust he will handle our vanity cases carefully."

She bestowed an angelic smile upon the hotel manager. Then, squandering a week's supply of poise on one regal gesture, she swept Natalie ahead of her into the old touring car. Roger

Gates was left behind on the curb to oversee the disposition of a dozen suitcases.

"Shame on you! That's hitting below the belt," Natalie hissed.

"But necessary!" Denise joined her in a muffled laugh. "After all, he did start it — wisecracking about our illustrious reputations. Just because his own career has suffered a setback gives him no right to downgrade the abilities of others."

The Cartugan driver wrestled with the heavier suitcases while Roger Gates hoisted the lighter pieces of luggage into the front of the car. Everything fit except the bulky bag of golf clubs. At last, Gates tossed it to the floor of the back seat with an offhand remark that it would be out of the way there.

This done, he climbed in beside the girls. "Shall I tie a white handkerchief to my putting iron, or is a mere apology sufficient?" he asked whimsically. "I solemnly swear to mind my manners in the future, but I do insist that you stop chucking suitcases at me."

"Consider yourself lucky, sir, that we came by air and therefore had no steamer trunks which required lifting!" But Denise ended the sentence with a giggle, unable to keep the severity in her tone one instant longer. Roger Gates appeared to have learned his lesson!

Their car jerked forward just as Luana de Cortez and her journalistic convoy arrived at the curb, trailed by the mob of noisy young "helpers." Glancing back through the rear window, Denise saw Leon Perdigo perform a courtly bow over the star's outstretched hand. Chivalry, at least in Cartuga, she thought, was undergoing a Renaissance.

Natalie's easy-going friendliness took up the slack in the conversation. "You speak beautiful Spanish," she told Roger Gates. "Are you well acquainted with the Caribbean?"

"Part of it," he said. "After my accident, I spent several months recuperating in Jamaica."

He paused, as though meaning to add something else, but at that moment the car turned away from the crowded city streets and bounced onto a picturesque rural road. Denise's murmur of pleasure forestalled any other remarks he might have intended to make. She swiveled from right to left, avidly absorbing every colorful detail of the countryside. Bougainvillea, cascaded from the sides of houses; dark, shiny-foliaged wild flowers encroached even onto the roadside. An overwhelming awareness of the tropics smote her as their route snaked through lush foothills. She gasped aloud at the sheer beauty of the scene when the mountain on one side fell away to reveal a creamy expanse of sand rolling down to the surf-capped ocean.

"Oh, look!"

Natalie pointed to a magnificent edifice of glass and willowy steel which soared eight stories tall above a wide, sheltered lagoon. One tiny islet floated decoratively a few hundred yards offshore, almost a reflection of the mainland vista. The waters lapping the sugar-white beach were blue beyond description.

"The Caribe Azure. What an ideal name!"

"Perfect!" Denise sighed, and Roger Gates chimed an appreciative comment. The trio sat quietly, almost mesmerized by the lavishness with which Nature had endowed this coastal region, until the car wound its way through a maze of lanes and creaked to a stop in one of the rear driveways.

Although the hotel was not yet officially open, its employees appeared to be extraordinarily busy. Gardeners were industriously planting a final row of blooms in the courtyard, construction workers hammered nails into latticework trellises, while teetering high above a regiment of window washers rubbed and polished until eight stories of glass glistened like sheets of diamonds.

Roger helped the girls alight onto the pebbled terrace. The driver whistled for porters to unload the mound of luggage. Even before the suitcases had been whisked away, the three athletes were being greeted by yet another representative of the hotel.

"Hello, I'm Vince Borden." A tall, slender young man with fair hair and a well tailored suit to match his Madison Avenue accent strode out to pump their hands. "Public Relations Director. And I must say," he added, his eyes reverting to Natalie after a polite second's rest on Roger and Denise, "that keeping this place in the headlines is going to be more fun than ever, now that the sports contingent has arrived."

"Why all the feverish activity?" Denise inquired. "I've always heard that islanders take life easily — even indolently."

"Not this week. Cartuga's President, Jorge Miras, has agreed to attend the opening festivities day after tomorrow, and Senor Lorrimer is determined to have the last detail finished by then." Vince Borden turned to the golfer and indicated a path leading to the opposite side of the courtyard. "Men's quarters in the west wing, Gates. Straight on back. I'll check to make sure you're comfortable after I turn the girls over to Mama Elena."

"Who?" Natalie asked.

He led them along a leafy arcade and into a long, low-slung auxiliary building. Even here in the employees' sector, the rooms were cool and high-ceilinged.

"She's head housekeeper for the hotel — and a self-styled *duenna* for all the girls who live here. Actually her name is Senora Valquez, but everyone here calls her Mama Elena. You'll love her!" Vince promised.

And the moment Denise set eyes on the motherly, middle-aged woman, she knew that this would be true. "Mama Elena" was short and amply proportioned. Black braids coiled high atop her head. A mirthful chuckle seemed to simmer just beneath her capable exterior.

"Didn't I tell you she was a sweetheart?" The public relations man gave Senora Valquez an affectionate squeeze.

"Get on back to your propaganda work," the housekeeper told him, pleased but unimpressed by his flattery. "*Vaya!* No men allowed down this hall, and you know it!"

With exaggerated alacrity, Vince Borden scooted out the door. A moment later, though, his head popped back around the frame. "I'll be lurking outside, waiting for my first tennis lesson!"

Denise giggled as Natalie blushed. "Looks as though you made a conquest," she observed.

The housekeeper, who had led the way down the wide, polished corridor, turned, smiling. "That Vincent — scatterbrained, oh my! But such a nice boy. Too bad I am not twenty years younger!"

Her black eyes crinkling with humor, she unlocked two doors near the end of the wing, and as proudly as if she were the owner of all she surveyed, escorted the girls through the small suites each of them would occupy.

"How very lovely!" Denise enthusiastically admired the sitting room, bedroom and bath which comprised her private quarters. "And so tastefully decorated. Those heavenly blue and green tones would make even the hottest day seem cool!"

Their luggage had been sent in ahead. Mama Elena departed, murmuring that she would give them time to become settled before showing them the way to the employees' dining hall.

But well before dinnertime she returned with a summons for Denise. "Senor Lorrimer has telephoned. He would be pleased to see you in his office now, if this is convenient."

Denise's heart pumped a little faster. It had been rash, signing a year's contract to work for a man she had never met. She knew nothing at all about him. Wavering, she reminded herself that the decision had been made weeks ago. Now she was duty-bound to carry through her agreement.

Nevertheless, it was with some trepidation that she entered the main building. In a less apprehensive mood she would have been drawn to the enchanting little specialty shops which dotted the first floor and ringed the sumptuous lobby. But her eyes flicked unseeingly past the resort-wear boutique and the jeweler's well-filled window; she barely noticed the display room filled with hand-made examples of Cartuga's famous wood-carving industry.

The office she sought lay in a quiet section of the building. The door stood ajar; it swung open at her timid knock.

"M-Mr. Lorrimer?"

The deference accorded his name wherever it was spoken, the awe in which he was held by Customs inspectors and porters alike, had prepared her to meet an entirely different type of person. From the advance build-up, Denise had expected him to be a grizzled tycoon, a giant who wore his success like a suit of armor and proceeded to gain his own ends with machine-like efficiency.

Instead, the man behind the desk was slim and small. His appearance clashed with the thoroughly American name he bore; his hair and eyes were dark, as was the well-tended mustache which adorned his upper lip. In the expensively cut riding clothes he favored he looked to be about forty, and she might have taken him for any upper-class islander whose blood was predominantly Spanish.

"Miss O'Shea?"

With formal courtesy Martin Lorrimer inquired about the comfort of her flight to Cartuga, the suitability of her quarters. Belatedly, it occurred to Denise that this wealthy, influential man had probably suffered the same misgivings about their meeting as she had. To him, she was an unknown quantity — a semi-celebrity who might prove to be rude, demanding or temperamental. At least in a small way, the very reputation of his hotel would depend upon her behavior. He had, she realized now, taken an even greater risk in offering that contract than she had in signing it!

Her tension ebbed. "I have visited many beautiful places, but the grandeur of the Hotel Caribe Azure and its surroundings outshines them all," she told him sincerely, almost unconsciously adopting the flowery form of speech which the Latin people used so eloquently. "I feel that I shall be truly happy here. Please tell me what my duties will be."

Martin Lorrimer responded with a hearty laugh. "You are to keep my guests from drowning! Of course," he added, "should someone arrive who knows nothing about the water, I would appreciate your giving a few simple lessons. Generally, however, you will merely be required to see that nobody goes under for the third time."

He arose impulsively, offering her his arm. "I should like very much to show you the 'crowning glory of my crowning glory.' As you may know, I have other hotel interests, but this" — an expansive gesture encompassed the masses of flowers, the towering structure of steel and glass — "this is my supreme accomplishment. There must be nothing but the best for the Caribe Azure."

Crossing under an archway decked with fragrant, trailing jasmine, he halted. "The pool, naturally, was built to championship specifications. I felt that it was only fitting for a champion to reign here."

Denise halted in astonished delight. Any water lover would be in his element here. Olympic sized, constructed with a symmetrical grace which echoed Martin Lorrimer's "nothing but the best" credo, the pool suggested a blue oasis shimmering amidst a desert of tiny white and coral tiles. But more amazing still was the lifeguard's chair. More like a throne than a lookout perch, it was adorned with massive reproductions of a gilt medallion. A tribute to the gold medal she had won!

"All this, and a salary too?" she gasped.

"You like it, then? Good!" A glow of pleasure lit his sensitive face. "Spending even a few days here at the Caribe Azure will be quite a costly investment for most people," the hotel owner explained his reasoning. "If, in addition to the finest accommodations and cuisine and a superb view, my guests can boast of a speaking acquaintance with one of America's swimming champions — well, undoubtedly they will consider their money well spent. And they may wish to recommend the hotel to their friends."

Senor Lorrimer mentioned that two island youths had also been engaged as assistant lifeguards, and duty hours could be arranged among the three of them.

Denise cast another look at the reflections dancing in the limpid waters of the pool. Should she pinch herself?

But her imagination was not capable of conjuring up such glories. It was all really, spectacularly true — and her job here promised to be twice as delightful as any career described in a book of fairy tales!

Chapter Three

That evening after dinner Denise and Natalie invited Mama Elena to accompany them on a "familiarization tour" around the hotel and its spacious grounds. The housekeeper cheerfully agreed to act as their guide. While escorting them through the various wings of the Caribe Azure she mentioned a number of unique local customs. She also pointed out a large bulletin board in the employees' recreation lounge which was reserved for the posting and explanation of news items of national importance.

A headline caught Denise's eyes. It dealt with proposed legislation which would allow all citizens above the age of eighteen to vote. After translating this from Spanish to English for Natalie's benefit, she turned to Mama Elena with a query.

"Cartuga hasn't always been a democracy, has it?"

"No, indeed." Senora Valquez shook her crown of braids. "Democracy, freedom — these very words are new to my countrymen."

In the past, she explained, a dynasty of brutal dictators had ruled the island. They oppressed the populace and exploited the laboring class to enrich their own already overflowing coffers.

Then, inevitably, rebellion had occurred.

"It was Jorge Miras who sparked the first flame of revolt," Mama Elena told the girls. "He was a University professor, not a soldier. Aided by a few heroic compatriots he led an organized movement of opposition against the dictator. All but a tiny percentage of the population was staunchly behind the rebellion. Even so, the army and the treasury were controlled by the tyrant. A tragic civil war was necessary to bring about reform." A fierce look of pride came into her eyes. "But the final victory was ours! And even though the fight against poverty has just begun, Cartuga is at last worthy of the name 're-public!'"

Cartuga, she added, had recently been accepted as a member of the Organization of American States. With the assistance of nations from both North and South America, the little democracy had embarked upon a grass-roots campaign against the disease and illiteracy which for generations had plagued her people.

Denise mentally compared Cartuga's history to that of Cuba. She found many points of similarity. But instead of replacing dictatorship with Communism, these courageous people had embraced democracy with a fervor unmatched since 1776.

"Jorge Miras must be a remarkable leader," she acknowledged.

"On the day after tomorrow you will have the opportunity of hearing this great man speak in person," Senora Valquez beamed excitedly at the girls. "He has consented to take part in the opening ceremonies of the hotel."

"I hope someone saves us ringside seats!" Natalie exclaimed.

A furrow creased itself between Denise's black brows. Jorge Miras here — in this setting of opulence? Somehow it seemed not quite fitting. There existed an appalling contrast between the luxurious atmosphere of the Caribe Azure and the austerity prevalent throughout the rest of the island. Why, she wondered, would a dedicated national leader consent to join in the frivolous opening day revelry, when a thousand more pressing tasks must surely vie for his attention?

Wisely, she kept these perplexing thoughts to herself. As they strolled out of doors into the balmy night air, the conversation left the area of politics and centered around Martin Lorrimer.

Mama Elena furnished several biographical sidelights about the hotel owner. His late father, she told the girls, had been an American; his mother was Cartugan.

Denise listened, engrossed. This explained the seeming incongruity between his appearance and his name; between the Yankee enterprise with which the hotel had been erected, and its owner's polished Spanish manners.

Despite his wealth, Martin Lorrimer sounded like a lonely man. Three years ago his wife had died, leaving him childless. A few months later his young sister had suddenly eloped with a man the family considered undesirable, and she had been killed in an automobile accident soon afterwards. Only his mother remained.

Before the girls could ask any further questions, a young man crossing the lawn detoured over to join their group. Vince Borden stretched a friendly arm around Mama Elena's shoulders, but his eyes quickly focused on Natalie.

"Seeing the sights?" he asked, belatedly including Denise in his smile of greeting. "You really ought to get a close look at the Caribbean before the shoreline becomes littered with tourists. Would you three ladies allow me to escort you on a stroll along the beach?"

"My legs were made for dancing, not walking," Mama Elena chuckled. "Not tonight, Vincent, thank you."

Denise also offered a prompt excuse. Her inclusion in the invitation had been a mere courtesy. Obviously, the handsome young public relations man desired only a better acquaintanceship with her friend.

She said goodnight and sauntered back toward her own quarters. She glanced over her shoulder once, but the sight of the two blond heads close together in the moonlight caused her to hasten her steps.

"Darn Tim anyway!"

Was the memory of his defection destined to forever warp her outlook on romance, Denise wondered. She tossed her dark head, reining in the runaway emotions. Plenty of girls had weathered broken engagements. The years ahead would provide ample opportunities for sentiment. Right now she had a job to do!

Morning, however, brought the reminder that, for the time being, she was a lifeguard without any lives to guard. The first stream of guests would not begin cascading into the Caribe Azure until after the opening day ceremonies tomorrow. Today her time was her own. She resolved to make good use of it.

Natalie groaned a muffled "go away" to Denise's perky invitation to sightsee. Between yawns, she emphasized that until some amateur tennis addict came beating upon the door with his racquet, it was her intention to remain sinfully slothful.

Denise felt secretly relieved that her invitation had been refused. She wanted to become familiar with every inch of this lovely island. Having to make conversation with another American might have impeded her progress in finding out what the people of Cartuga were really like. She practiced her still-halting Spanish on the waiter who served her breakfast, then borrowed one of the bicycles kept for use by members of the hotel staff and happily pointed the handlebars in the direction of San Marco.

There was little motorized traffic, but other cyclists and pedestrians thronged the crushed-shell road. Denise was enchanted by the sight of women swinging cheerfully along, nonchalantly balancing laden bowls of fruit on their heads in the age-old manner of islanders going to market. Without exception, the women were colorfully dressed, and Denise, clad in plaid slacks, a red shirt, and a bright scarf tied over her head, felt a merry kinship with them. She smiled impartially at everyone she passed. Oddly enough, very few of the people smiled back, and to her bewilderment she detected a number of almost scandalized glances in her direction.

But even this could not mar her enjoyment of the ride. The midday heat was still hours away, the scent of blossoms fragrant without being overpowering, and glimpses through the dense foliage of quaint, other-worldish villages heightened her sense of embarking on an adventurous new experience.

After passing what appeared to be a well-to-do residential suburb on the outskirts of the city, she ventured into San Marco proper. Following the crowds, she came upon a huge, open marketplace where stacks of hand-made pottery, implements and serving dishes carved from wood, and bins of garden produce stood side-by-side with stands where Cartugan specialties were sizzling on griddles.

Denise walked her bike slowly past the stalls of merchandise, marveling at the wide assortment of articles for sale. While she managed to resist the tantalizing aromas wafting her way, she did purchase a few small trinkets. For these she was required to bargain, an exhilarating game entered into with gusto by the vendors on the one hand, and in groping but determined Spanish on her part. Again she noticed the peculiar, side-long glances darted at her by nearly everyone she encountered, but until she had retraced her route along the roadside, almost devoid of traffic now, the reason for this remained unexplained.

Midway between the city and the hotel, at a juncture of roads serving a tiny community of ramshackle homes, she happened across a crew of workmen. Here she was forced to halt while brawny, perspiring men wrestled a huge length of pipe across the lane and lowered it carefully into a muddy ditch several feet below the grade.

Off to one side a jeep was parked. It was hardly large enough to have conveyed both the pipe and the team of laborers to the site, however, and she couldn't help wondering whether the men could possibly have transported the heavy tube from the city with their bare hands. It seemed an impossible task.

She was still waiting for the obstruction to be cleared when a couple of the workmen glanced in her direction. A grin split the face of one of the men. Without bothering to lower his voice, he made a remark to his companion.

Denise's ears burned. At that moment she almost wished that she *didn't* understand Spanish!

"These crazy foreign women — riding around the streets in men's clothing," was a rough translation of his comment.

The second man raised his head. Cool, interested grey eyes met hers. Met, and held for a long, embarrassed half-minute.

A surge of hot, angry color flooded her cheeks. Furiously, Denise kicked off the brake. Her strong, swimmer's legs sent the bike racing past the gang of workmen.

"Hey, wait a minute!" she heard someone call. In accents about as Spanish as a peanut-butter sandwich. Or chocolate chip ice-cream. "Hold on! He didn't mean —" The rest was lost, choked off in the dusty smoke-screen stirred up by her churning wheels.

So he was an American, she thought heatedly. Even though he was nearly as tan as the natives. A fine thing, one of her own countrymen —

In justice, she reassigned the blame. *He,* the one with the cool, appraising grey eyes, hadn't made the crack. His companion had, obviously not expecting crazy foreign women to understand Spanish. *He* had only looked — but with a deliberating stare which had seemed to echo agreement.

Denise's face flared with a new wave of color. No wonder every second person she had met that morning had looked at her askance! She glanced down at the dusty plaid of her slacks. Men's clothing, indeed! But even a free, democratic Cartuga might have its taboos, and apparently here women dressed decorously in skirts at all times. One of the quaint, local customs Mama Elena had forgotten to mention, no doubt!

By the time she reached the grounds of the hotel her fury had cooled. She was even able to smile a bit at the humor of the situation. It was a tight smile, though. Pedaling around the island in slacks was a mistake she would never repeat!

All that day a growing air of excitement pervaded the Hotel Caribe Azure. Denise noticed that the frenzied activity to have each finishing touch in place for the grand opening ceremonies was even more marked than had been evident upon their arrival. The undercurrent of anticipation was especially strong in the staff quarters, where wide-eyed housemaids and waiters reported upon the arrival of each new contingent of newspapermen. Scores of them seemed to be already in residence, along with a handful of top entertainers who would add their famous names and talents to publicizing this latest resort jewel on the shores of the Caribbean.

"What? No boy friend in attendance?" Denise joked, when Natalie asked her to join in a set of tennis the next morning.

"Vince? He's the busiest little bee that ever flew out of a hive," Natalie dimpled. "It's his job to keep those hordes of travel writers happy until after the official ribbon-cutting ceremonies this noon. When I saw him last night he was practically limping, poor lamb. Escorting groups of them on tours around the island is a pretty exacting task." She lobbed the ball complacently over the net. "I don't mind, though. I have a hunch he'll be getting back to me as soon as all this hoop-la quiets down."

Denise bounced across the court in quest of a stinging drive from Natalie's racquet. She put up a valiant battle, but soon realized that she was no match for the tiny blonde champion.

"Whew! That's enough," she cried, after forty-five minutes of muscle-straining activity. "Another lunge like that last one, and I'll land flat on my face." She tossed her racquet aside, laughing good-naturedly in defeat. "You'll have to let me challenge you to a swimming match one of these days so I can save face."

Natalie gave a delicate shudder. "Water has always terrified me," she confided. "My twin sister drowned when we were about five years old. Since then — Really, I'm not even comfortable in a bathtub."

Denise was instantly contrite. "Oh, Nat, I didn't mean to resurrect unhappy memories for you. I'm sorry." After a pause she added hesitantly, "Swimming is more than a sport, you know. Everyone ought to know a few rudimentary strokes, if only for their own protection. If you should ever decide that you want to learn, I'll be glad to teach you."

"Well, maybe one of these days," Natalie promised vaguely. She glanced at the ornamental sundial adjacent to the courts. "Gracious, it's past eleven o'clock. We'll have to hurry if we are to shower and change before all the celebrities start arriving. Vince said he would try to arrange an introduction to President Miras for us. I'm dying to meet him, aren't you?"

"He sounds like an interesting person," Denise said.

She gathered together her possessions, and followed Natalie up the winding path. Yes, she decided, she *would* like to meet the man responsible for the revolution which had made Cartuga a republic. She only hoped that the legendary hero would not prove to be a disappointment. On her ride into San Marco the previous day she had had a first-hand glimpse of the grim conditions existing on the island. Now, more than ever, Cartuga needed a leader of integrity and valor.

Denise smiled self-consciously to herself. All of a sudden she seemed to have developed a social conscience. She supposed it was because, here, deprivation was more the rule than the exception. A confrontation with so much real need was enough to make anyone think twice about his own good fortune.

Back in her room, Denise slipped quickly into and out of the shower, then donned a crisp linen sheath. Vivid colors had always suited her raven-black locks and fair complexion; the coral tones of the dress and its matching high-heeled sandals were especially flattering. She skimmed a powder puff across her nose, dabbed on lipstick of a complementary hue, and stepped back to appraise her appearance in the mirror.

Natalie saved her the trouble. "What a stunning outfit!" she exclaimed, popping her head into the room.

The petite blonde girl wore a lemony-yellow dress accented by white accessories. The ensemble was perfect for her diminutive figure.

"You look like a nice, fresh daisy yourself," Denise smiled. "Let's hurry, shall we? I'm sure everyone else has already gone down to the pavilion."

They hastened through the empty building and down the arcade which bordered the main edifice. An enormous crowd had already gathered in the wide terrace adjoining the pool. By standing on tiptoe the girls could glimpse the assembled dignitaries already seated on a temporary stage.

Martin Lorrimer had discarded his jodhpurs in favor of more formal attire. Denise shaded her eyes, her attention drawn to the lean, white-haired man whom the hotel owner was ceremoniously introducing. His craggy features would never have graced a movie screen, but even from this distance she could sense the tremendous magnetism of the man. Jorge Miras? Her guess was confirmed by the burst of applause which swelled to a ringing ovation as he stepped to the microphone.

Cartuga's President spoke in Spanish, but his phrasing was leisurely enough so that Denise was able to mentally translate almost all of the speech into English as he went along. She interpreted in a whisper for Natalie.

"He's saying what a boon this hotel will be to the Cartugan people," she murmured. "Several hundred families will benefit directly through salaries paid for working at the hotel. The island's economy as a whole will be raised through the expected influx of tourists and the money they spend here."

A sense of relief stole over her as she remembered that she had not expressed aloud the disquieting ideas which had occurred to her on the evening of her arrival. At that time the hotel had seemed to her almost an affront to the Cartugan people — a few luxurious acres which contrasted appallingly with the hardship and privation so prevalent throughout the rest of the island. Now, however, the words of President Miras led her to realize that the establishment of Martin Lorrimer's plush resort might in time actually help to abolish some of the cruel poverty she had noticed.

She bent to whisper in Natalie's ear as the speech came to an end. "What a magnificent speaker! No wonder he inspired the people to follow him during the revolution. He must —"

"Excuse me, please. May I get through?"

Denise turned at the light pressure on her shoulder, automatically moving aside to grant the request. The crowd in front of her, however, was more grudging in its response. Glancing upwards, Denise saw a rather tall young man clad in formal afternoon attire. His eyes were fastened impatiently on the distant podium, but as she took in various details of his appearance — the crisp, wavy brown hair, the deep tan which marked him as an outdoor man — he cast a harried look over his shoulder. Denise found herself gazing into the same penetrating grey eyes which had met hers from the depths of that muddy roadside ditch.

The memory of that brief encounter still stung. "At affairs such as this, it's wise to come early if you expect a seat up front," she remarked coolly.

A ghost of a smile tugged at his lips. "You're so right!" he acknowledged, before thrusting his way through the dense throng ahead of them.

Natalie hadn't missed the exchange. "Who on earth was that?"

"I haven't the faintest idea," Denise shrugged.

"Then you're sadly uninformed," said Vince Borden, coming up behind them. "That's John Westcott, Vice-Consul of the United States here in Cartuga." He grinned at Denise. "Maybe you two should get together. As a member of the diplomatic corps, he's considered a rather important person on the island!"

Chapter Four

Denise gaped at him, her mouth a small, round "O" of astonishment. Surely he didn't mean that the shirtless pipelayer of the ditch was actually a member of the diplomatic corps! Vice-Consul of the United States! Her imagination boggled at the idea. But when John Westcott rose from his chair on the platform to make a short speech a few minutes later, she was forced to accept the truth of Vince's statement.

A wave of mortification swept over her. What a gauche creature he must think her! As if it weren't bad enough that she had all but caused a scandal by bicycling around the island in slacks, she had to make matters worse by heckling him about his late arrival!

She groaned inwardly. "One of these days my big mouth is going to get me into real trouble!"

Looking back on his reaction, though, Denise remembered that he had been amused rather than angered by her ill-timed remark. At least she hoped that was the case. In any event, she didn't intend to give him a second chance to vent his irritation. She would arrange to make a wide detour around Mr. Westcott in the future!

The speech-making part of the ceremonies droned to a close. Dignitaries and onlookers alike drifted through the arcade to the pool area, where tables had been set up to provide refreshments for the throng. Denise spotted numerous already-familiar faces, and waved to Roger Gates who was chatting with Mama Elena on the opposite side of the pavilion. Vince excused himself briefly after seeing that the girls were supplied with canapes I and frosty glasses of fruit punch. They were crestfallen when he reappeared with the news that Jorge Miras had already departed to attend a Government conference, but were somewhat mollified by his promise to introduce them to the President at a later date.

A native Calypso band sauntered around the outskirts of the pavilion, pausing now and then to entertain the various groups of people. The outrageously funny lyrics of their songs soon had Denise and Natalie giggling. Caught up in the music and laughter around her, Denise felt her mood relax. Eventually the crowd began to thin, and when Natalie and Vince were buttonholed by a trio of magazine reporters she decided that it was time she, too, left the party.

"Oh, Miss O'Shea!"

Denise paused, one foot on the pebbled path, and turned to see Martin Lorrimer advancing toward her. Her color heightened at the sight of the young man he had in tow. John Westcott!

Oh, no! she thought dismally.

There was, oddly enough, no sign of displeasure on the hotel owner's face. "Miss O'Shea, this gentleman has requested the pleasure of your acquaintance," he smiled. "May I present Mr. John Westcott, a most distinguished representative of your own country. Mr. Westcott, Miss Denise O'Shea."

Denise extended her hand as she collected her scattered wits, and murmured a polite reply. So he hadn't tattled, after all!

"I feel that you two young people will find that you share many common interests." The hotel magnate hastily excused himself to tend to his duties as a host.

There was an awkward pause, filled only by the light-hearted refrain of a Calypso song wafting across the pavilion.

"Island woman always say
Worthless mahn you stay away
The mahn he say, don't talk so smart —
Island woman have no heart!"

Denise drew a deep breath. "I — I believe I owe you an apology. I was rude — I'm sorry."

"Like the 'Island woman' you 'talked too smart?'" A merry twinkle brightened his grey eyes. "You weren't rude, though — just forthright. I imagine it did look rather pushy, my elbowing my way through the crowd like that."

"Well, you might have *said* that you were expected on the speakers' platform," Denise complained.

"What? And have you term me a braggart?"

He laughed in genuine amusement. "Actually, I wasn't expected there — until about an hour ago. My boss was supposed to do the honors. But he slipped, coming down the steps of the Consulate, and wrenched his ankle. I was pushed into the line-up as a last-minute substitute." He grimaced wryly. "Speech-making isn't exactly my line of country."

"But pipe-laying is?"

"Oh, that." John Westcott didn't seem offended by the query. He took her elbow and steered her expertly through the milling crowd. "Have a bench, and I'll explain."

He seated himself beside Denise on the graceful, wrought-iron lounge. "You are now one of the few people who knows my deep, dark secret. You see, I worked with a construction crew to finance my way through college. When I came over here and saw the terrific need for sanitation facilities —" His broad shoulders shrugged expressively. "Well, the best way to teach someone a trade is to get in there and show them how to do the job. It seemed a shame to let all that practical experience go to waste."

"You've been training that crew of workmen?" Denise was impressed by the simplicity of his words. "It looked like an enormous project."

"It's a bit more difficult than if we had the heavy machinery we used in the States," he admitted. "The culverts had to be dug by hand, and the pipe hauled out piece by piece from San Marco in my jeep. But it will be more than worth the effort when we get the job finished. For the first time in history, the town of Soledad will be supplied with purified running water. Up until now the inhabitants have had only the community cistern to depend upon for every drop of water they use."

"Good heavens! I knew the islanders were poor, but I had no idea conditions were quite that primitive!" she exclaimed.

"We've a long way to go. But we are making some progress." Abruptly, he changed the subject. "Senor Lorrimer mentioned that you are to be head lifeguard here at the Caribe Azure. Did you take Spanish lessons before you came?"

Denise guessed that this was an oblique reference to the scene which had occurred at the construction site.

"At home in California we have a large Spanish-speaking population. Most schools include the language as part of the curriculum. I used to practice on whomever would listen, but I'm still far from fluent, unfortunately." She dimpled, her embarrassed recollection of the incident softened by his friendliness. "Perhaps I should have made a study of Cartugan customs, as well. I had no idea I would scandalize anyone by wearing slacks."

He nodded sympathetically. "It isn't easy to adopt the customs of a new country overnight. I'm only sorry you learned that one the hard way. Felipe, of course, didn't realize you spoke the language. The people here are almost painfully polite. They would never deliberately hurt another person's feelings."

A splatter of large, totally unexpected raindrops forestalled Denise's reply. She jumped to her feet with an indignant exclamation. "For heaven's sakes — there isn't a cloud in the sky!"

"I'm afraid you'll have to get used to this aspect of Cartugan life, too," John Westcott laughed. "During the summer these showers are a regular, twice-a-day affair. The other seasons aren't quite so predictable." He glanced hastily around in search of shelter. Finding none close by, he grasped her elbow and guided her quickly beneath the arcade's overhang.

Seconds later, the deluge struck with full force. Raindrops the size of half dollars tattooed the ground and rattled the palm fronds with a vibrating intensity. Peering through the crystal curtain of rain, Denise saw that the pavilion had emptied in record time, most of the remaining guests having made a wild dash for the hotel at the first sign of a downpour. Only one other person had sought the shelter of the arcade ahead of them.

Roger Gates arched an impudent red-brown eyebrow at the hurrying pair. "Thought you liked the water!"

"I do — in concentrated supply. Not a drop at a time," Denise returned. She introduced the two men. The threesome chatted idly for a few minutes longer. When the torrent began to abate, John Westcott excused himself to keep an appointment in San Marco.

Watching him stride back across the damp courtyard, Denise wondered if he might have lingered longer, had they not been interrupted. He had seemed to enjoy her company, yet he had said nothing about seeing her again. A vision of Tim rose unbidden to her mind. She gave a tiny shrug. It had been a pleasant interlude, nothing more. And perhaps, for the moment, that was just as well.

With the initial ceremonies over, the hotel opened its doors for business in earnest. Guests flocked to the Caribe Azure — planeloads of them from New York and Philadelphia and other chilly Northern cities, while a lesser but equally enthusiastic number of visitors disembarked from cruise ships plying the Caribbean to spend a day or two at the fabulous new luxury resort.

Denise found the pair of native boys with whom she shared the lifeguard duties to be excellent swimmers. This was no more than she had expected, knowing Martin Lorrimer's exacting standards. Alfonso and Jose were lithe, agile youths, who could knife through the water with the speed of eels when a cry for help sounded from any part of the gigantic pool.

This seldom happened. The majority of tourists preferred to splash in the frothing shoreline surf, or to stretch out on cushions along the wide, mosaic-tile terrace ringing the pool to toast in the golden sun. There were more cases of sunburn than near drownings among the hotel clientele. Nevertheless, Denise and her fellow lifeguards kept constantly on the alert in case a swimmer should get out of his depth, or develop a sudden cramp.

The interest displayed in the three champion athletes was a tribute to Martin Lorrimer's business acumen. People who had never before played tennis were encouraged by Natalie's deceptively fragile appearance to try the game. They left the courts with blisters worn by the unaccustomed grip of the racquet, but her bubbling personality and thorough knowledge of the sport usually drew them back for more lessons as soon as the blisters had healed.

Denise had left her gold medal at home in California, but even without the unmistakable replicas of the award adorning her lifeguard perch, she was easily recognizable to most of the guests. An increasing number of them shyly requested her help in perfecting their strokes.

Nor was Roger Gates ignored by the tourists. The manicured, eighteen-hole golf course adjoining the Caribe Azure had already been favorably compared to some of the world's most noted greens. Denise's father was not the only "incurable golf buff" familiar with Roger's prowess on the links. His appointment book soon overflowed with names of hotel visitors eager to boast to friends back home that they had been given golf lessons by such a distinguished "pro."

Denise was quick to notice the change this revival of interest by his former fans brought about in Roger. The chip on his shoulder when he arrived in Cartuga had been large enough to use as tinder for a bonfire. However, once he realized that the back injury which kept him from competing in the major golf classics did not detract from the fame of his earlier exploits, his personality mellowed.

Natalie encountered Denise en route to the employees' dining room one morning, and strolled in to breakfast with her. "I knew you were an early riser, but this is ridiculous!" She hid a yawn behind her coffee cup. Eyeing her friend's lightweight blue suit and high-heeled shoes, she remarked, "I thought this was your day off. Don't you ever sleep?"

"Certainly. But at night, not on such beautiful mornings as this," Denise replied. "Look at all that glorious sunshine! Can you believe that Christmas is only two weeks away?"

Natalie groaned. "I'm trying not to think of it. I haven't done a lick of shopping yet. There doesn't seem to be a moment to spare around here —"

"To spare from work, or to spare from Vince?" Denise laughed and glanced at her wristwatch before slicing into the juicy crescent of papaya on her plate. "If you have any definite gifts in mind, I could pick them up for you in San Marco this morning. Roger has hired a car and is driving me in."

"Roger Gates? I thought you didn't like him."

"Well, I didn't, at first," Denise confessed. "But I'm pretty sure that antagonistic manner of his was only a cover-up. He was afraid everyone would think of him as a has-been, and it hurt his pride." She lowered her voice. "I found out yesterday that his wife was killed in the same accident that injured him so badly. They had been married only a few days. A double blow like that would be enough to sour anyone."

"Oh, the poor man!" Soft-hearted Natalie was instantly sympathetic. "Who told you about that?"

"My bedroom door was open, and I overheard Mama Elena gossiping with Catalina Ruiz in the hall."

Denise set her napkin on the table, and picked up her smart, alligator-skin handbag. "Let's not repeat this to anyone else. He probably came over here to try and forget his heartaches, not to be reminded of them. How about your shopping? I can look around the market for you, if you'd like me to."

Natalie mentioned that her Aunt Florence was especially fond of unusual jewelry. "If you run across any outstanding bracelets or earrings, get a set for me. I'll pay you tonight."

Denise promised to see what she could find. Roger was already waiting in the parking lot when she hurried out the side entrance. She widened her smile for his benefit, thinking that she had never seen him look so carefree.

"Is this the Santa Claus express?" she teased.

"How did you guess?" Sunlight dappled his red-brown hair as he leaned across to open the car door for her. "I'm convinced that reindeer instead of horses furnish the power for this heap. At that, it's the pick of Honest Hernando's used car lot." He started the wheezy engine. "If Detroit ever hears about Cartuga, they'll rig up an extra assembly line."

It was true that comparatively few motorized vehicles existed on the island. "I doubt that many people here could afford even a second-hand car," Denise said, remembering the town of Soledad which still depended on the community well. And John Westcott had assured her that it was one of the island's more progressive towns!

The ancient car covered the distance into San Marco smoothly enough, though, and they spent a happy four hours wandering through the city's shops and markets. Denise found colorful, hand-loomed blankets which she decided would make excellent gifts for her grandmother and a newly-married cousin. At a silversmith's she ran across bracelets and earrings of a lacy, filigree design. She bought a set for her mother, and a duplicate set for Natalie's aunt. Diligent searching unearthed other examples of native handicraft which made original presents for her father and several friends at home. Then, above Roger's protests that the reindeer would mutiny, she bartered for a huge woven straw basket in which to cram all her purchases.

"I really appreciate your taking the time to go with me," she told him, as they alighted from the car and walked back to the staff's quarters. "It would have been mighty hard to balance all this stuff on the handlebars of my bicycle!"

"Glad to help out," Roger smiled. "See you at the party on the 24th."

"We can sing the English version of the carols, while everyone else is warbling in Spanish," Denise promised.

For the first time since her arrival in Cartuga, she was experiencing a bout of homesickness. The gaily-wrapped packages which arrived from California during the next incongruously balmy weeks were poignant reminders of her far-away home and family. But a brief visit with her parents by way of a wickedly expensive telephone call cheered her, and she was in a holiday mood when she and Roger joined the hundreds of other hotel employees in a joyous celebration of the Nativity. Each person brought along a small gift, and the exchanging of these led to much laughter and a happy feeling of fellowship among the American and Cartugan members of the staff.

After attending Mass on Christmas Day, she joined with the other employees of the Caribe Azure in organizing a festive gala for the hotel guests.

While most vactioners could afford to spend only a few days at the plush Caribbean resort, there were some to whom expense was of no concern. Most of these guests were elderly ladies with whom Denise seldom came into contact. Myra Hendricks was an exception. Twice each day Mrs. Hendricks doggedly swam the length of the pool and back, after which she would retire to a solitary chaise lounge on the terrace. She had been at the Caribe Azure almost since its opening, but appeared to have made few friends among the other residents.

"She and her husband are of the 'new rich.' Those whose ancestors made their fortunes do not easily accept her into their exclusive little circle," Mama Elena, who always seemed to know everything about everybody, had commented, when Denise inquired about the woman. "The old friends, who are still poor, are overawed by so much money," the housekeeper philosophized, "and those who have always been rich look down on her. It is sad."

It *was* sad. In spite of all her husband's money, Denise felt rather sorry for Mrs. Hendricks. Her hair seemed to be forever wisping out of its fashionable chignon, and not even the chic Paris wardrobe could conceal the unstylish rotundity of her figure. Denise fell into the habit of exchanging a few words with the woman whenever she was on duty at the pool. Mrs. Hendricks appeared pathetically grateful for this offer of friendship. Occasionally, she would draw her chair up next to the lifeguard perch and chat for an hour or more. But the long-term residents continued to snub her, and the transient vacationers were too busy sightseeing or indulging in vigorous sports to offer any companionship to a lonely, middle-aged woman.

So at the party Denise, who had been performing introductions and making sure that no guest was excluded from the holiday revelry, was both surprised and pleased to observe Mrs. Hendricks laughing and talking with a rugged, grey-haired man. The woman's eyes sparkled with vitality. Against the background of the lavishly decorated lounge she looked more youthful, and happiness had brought an attractive rosiness to her round face. When Mrs. Hendricks spotted Denise, she beckoned insistently.

"Come over here, dear, and meet my husband," she called. "Walter, this is Miss O'Shea. She has helped make my stay in Cartuga very happy."

Denise ignored the exaggeration. If Mrs. Hendricks wanted her husband to believe that the Caribbean vacation was a blissful experience, that was her business. She murmured a conventional phrase to Mr. Hendricks.

Who, she thought a moment later, was nobody's fool. He studied her gravely before extending his hand. "Myra often talks about you in her letters. Your being here has made all the difference in the world to her," he said forthrightly. "She wanted to come home two weeks ago, but the doctors wouldn't hear of it. Said with her bronchial condition, another severe

New York winter would kill her." He wrapped an arm fondly around his wife's plump shoulders. "I'm depending on you to keep her here in the sunshine until the Spring thaw."

"Now, Walter, don't you start fussing about me," Myra Hendricks chided. "Sit down, both of you. I want to show Denise my present."

Sinking down, Denise opened the impressive jeweler's box which was passed across to her. A gasp escaped her lips. Nestled amidst the creamy satin folds was the cotliest ornament she had ever seen. Rubies and emeralds were interlaced along a solid chain of square-cut diamonds. Held up to the light, the gems shimmered with a molten brilliance.

"How absolutely magnificent," she said faintly, aware that any attempted description of the necklace was bound to be a rank understatement.

Mrs. Hendricks looked pleased but at the same time slightly overcome by the splendid array of jewels. "It's grand, isn't it?" she laughed self-consciously. "I told Walter he should hang it on the Christmas tree, instead of on me."

"None of that, Mother! You'll look like a queen with that around your neck," Walter Hendricks declared proudly. "I want you to wear it every night. It's a shame I can't stay past New Years to see you keep on enjoying yourself."

Denise slipped away to let them enjoy their brief reunion. Now she understood why the lonely little woman had remained so long in

Cartuga. She had found Walter Hendricks' pride in his wife very touching. She could picture him scouring New York in search of a gift with which to compensate Myra for her enforced exile. Hopefully, her next winter vacation could be spent in more congenial surroundings.

The popularity of the Caribe Azure skyrocketed after the holiday season. With the influx of the international "jet set," the sports personnel's chores were doubled. Natalie acquired an assistant tennis coach; extra caddies were hired for duty on the golf course, and an additional lifeguard was set to work patrolling the hotel's private beach from dusk to midnight.

"Honestly, those people do the craziest things!" Natalie collapsed limply onto Denise's bed one evening early in February. "Today some woman challenged me to a blindfold match. Can you imagine? And how about that Italian count trying to dive off his fifth-story balcony into the pool?"

"I believe that sort of behavior is known as 'madcap,' " Denise said wryly. "Should one of them drown, or be smashed in the nose by a hard serve, we would probably be blamed."

But as it turned out, it was Myra Hendricks who almost drowned.

She was a competent swimmer and Denise, whose attention these days was riveted mainly on the frenzied poolside activity of the thrill-seeking international clique, had long ago ceased to worry when her friend approached the ten-foot depth. Apprehensively watching the antics of two youths on the high diving board, she missed the first panic-stricken splashes signaling danger in the center of the pool. But a terrified cry sent her eyes flashing across the water.

Trouble!

Denise catapulted into the water. With swift, fluid strokes she closed the distance between herself and Mrs. Hendricks. She screamed a warning to the swimmers blocking her path. Miraculously, they splashed aside in time to avert a collision. Her charming arms and legs pulled her even with the drowning woman just as Mrs. Hendricks floundered weakly and appeared to give up the struggle.

Denise jackknifed, thrusting her arms beneath the sinking form. Mrs. Hendricks bobbed to the surface. Her head lolled back in the water, cap off, her hair fanning out like greying wisps of seaweed. She sputtered and choked as air mingled with the water in her lungs. In a moment of panicky confusion she flailed out against her rescuer. Denise's superior strength triumphed, however. Her face was a mask of grim determination as she towed the woman over to the side, where willing arms waited to hoist them both out of the water.

Touch and go, Denise thought, expertly straddling Mrs. Hendricks' back while she kneaded the water from her lungs. Pulse slow — only half conscious . . . these thoughts raced through her mind. Why hadn't she been more alert? She shook the streaming hair out of her eyes and pumped. Up, down. Up, down. Denise shrugged aside someone's offer to take over the resuscitation process, continuing blindly until she heard the feeble gasp.

"Cramp . . . had a cramp."

Denise sank back on her heels, trembling in relief. The lifesaving technique had worked!

Myra Hendricks' face was a flaccid grey. But she had a resilient spirit, and soon managed to achieve a sitting position. After a few minutes' respite she was able to speak coherently.

"The most terrible pain — doubling up my legs. I couldn't make any headway at all. It was a dreadful experience. The only thing I could think of was that I would never see Walter again!" She smiled tremulously at Denise. "My dear, how can I ever express my thanks?"

"There is no need for you to even try." Anxiously, Denise added, "Do you feel strong enough to go inside now? I won't be able to relax until the doctor has had a look at you."

Mrs. Hendricks struggled to her feet, looking abashed at the furor she had created. "Piffle! I'm quite all right now." Even so, she leaned heavily on the girl's arm, and a slight limp impeded their progress.

Alfonso, who had been absent at the time of the near-tragedy, was left in charge of the pool. As she shepherded her friend into the hotel Denise noted thankfully that the clowning on the diving board had stopped, at least temporarily. She had been watching their silly stunts — She blanched at the thought of how serious a result the youths' capering high-jinks might have had!

Comfortably ensconced in her satin-covered bed, Mrs. Hendricks fidgeted while Denise put through a call to the hotel doctor.

"I couldn't bear to have anyone find me looking like this," she fretted. "Would you mind bringing over my comb and hairbrush — and that fluffy white bedjacket in the top bureau drawer? It's right there on top of my necklace," she directed, when Denise had trouble locating the garment.

Rummaging through the stacks of embroidered lingerie, Denise finally pulled out the bedjacket. A little frown puckered her brow. "I don't see any necklace here," she remarked hesitantly. "Do you mean the emerald and ruby choker your husband gave you for Christmas?"

Her eyes widened at Myra Hendricks' blithe nod. "But surely — you *do* usually keep it in the hotel safe, don't you?"

"Nonsense, child, that's such a bother. I wear it every night because Walter was so proud of it. Why should I traipse back and forth to the office every time I want to put on a piece of jewelry?"

She climbed out of bed and trudged over to the bureau. "I leave it right here with my slips and things, where nobody would think of bothering it."

Denise's concern burgeoned as she watched Mrs. Hendricks pat each item of lingerie, and finally empty the whole drawer out onto the bed. Silks, satins, laces littered the spread in filmy profusion. Their colors ran the gamut of the rainbow — blue, coral, yellow and chartreuse.

But of green emeralds and blood-red rubies there was no sign.

A mushroom cloud of tension suffocated the room. Leon Perdigo's office overflowed with people and sounds and an ominous atmosphere of mistrust. Denise stood near the door, belting a terrycloth jacket over her damp bathing suit, and tried to sort out the voices. It wasn't hard to distinguish Myra Hendricks' aggrieved Northern twang from the hotel manager's stilted basso, but Catalina Ruiz's protesting sobs blended incoherently with the calming noises made by Mama Elena.

"I tell you I *saw* the necklace in that drawer less than an hour before I went out for my swim!"

"This is a calamitous occurrence, Senora. The management of the Caribe Azure is desolate —"

"I did not take it! I did not touch so much as a finger to it! Ay, Mamacita —"

"Hush, child. Do not weep so. Nobody has accused you of stealing the necklace."

Denise shifted uncomfortably from one foot to the other, wishing she could escape. The scene had been going on for half an hour, and looked as if it might continue indefinitely. Clearly, Leon Perdigo wished to avoid involving the police, whose appearance could not help but trigger a scandal detrimental to the hotel. But he had summoned Catalina Ruiz, the maid in charge of cleaning that particular suite, after Mrs. Hendricks had indignantly announced that her necklace had been stolen. The hotel's head housekeeper, Mama Elena, was also called in. Denise's presence when the loss was discovered had included her in the distressing conference.

She chafed at the delay. "Poor Alfonso. He must think I'm playing hookey!"

Buffeted by alternate accusations and denials, Leon Perdigo at last arose and suggested that he make a personal search of the suite before appealing to the authorities.

"It is possible that the necklace has merely been mislaid," he said optimistically, guiding Mrs. Hendricks into an elevator. "The honesty of our employees has never been questioned. I would hesitate to endanger the reputation of Senorita Ruiz without first satisfying myself that the gems are nowhere to be found."

Denise couldn't help thinking that the matter would have been handled much less emotionally, had Martin Lorrimer been present. But the hotel owner was away on a business trip, and the burden had fallen onto his assistant's unwilling shoulders.

She squeezed Catalina's hand as they padded down the luxuriously carpeted hall. She and the shy, pretty maid had become friends during the past few months, and her heart ached for the girl's plight. Catalina was no thief! But nonetheless, an uneasy prickle of worry tiptoed up her spine. Who else knew about Mrs. Hendricks' carelessness? And who else, she thought with a gulp, could have managed to enter the locked suite?

The hotel manager painstakingly searched through the jumbled heap of garments on the bed before turning his attention to the other drawers of the bureau. An examination of those on top revealed nothing. But when he drew open the drawer directly below that which had contained the bedjacket, he uttered a triumphant exclamation.

"Behold the missing gems!"

Open-mouthed, Mrs. Hendricks clasped the necklace to her bosom. "But — I don't understand. How did it get down there?"

A grain of annoyance seeped through Leon Perdigo's obsequious facade. He shrugged.

"Gravity, no doubt. It sometimes happens that two boards are not solidly joined together." He indicated the empty drawer on the bed. "As you will observe, there is just such an imperfection here at the base. The necklace obviously slipped through the crack and dropped down to the second drawer."

He straightened up, poise and pompousness regained. "I shall see to it that this defective bureau is immediately replaced. However, for reasons of security, I suggest that in the future you store your jewels in the office safe."

"Oh, I will!" Myra Hendricks cried. "I feel terrible about having caused such a commotion." She looked humbly at Catalina, whose face was blotched and red from weeping. "Please forgive me, all of you."

Denise started to speak, then checked the words. No harm had been done, after all. Nothing but more confusion could result if she were to tell them that while Mrs. Hendricks was rummaging through the lingerie on the bed, she herself had opened the second drawer. And the necklace *hadn't* been there then!

No harm done, Denise thought again. But it was strange. Awfully strange!

Chapter Five

"The Case of the Momentarily Disappearing Necklace," as Denise privately termed the incident, made only a faint ripple in the placid pond of life as it was lived at the Caribe Azure.

Within a few days the matter had been practically forgotten. A twinge of apprehension still troubled her whenever she pondered the strange circumstances that had surrounded the episode, but since she could find no logical way of explaining the "now you see it, now you don't" affair, she prudently kept her suspicions to herself. Therefore, the only immediate results of the afternoon's scare were an increased caution on the part of Myra Hendricks, and the cementing of a firm friendship between Denise and Catalina Ruiz.

"I still tremble with fright when I think how close I came to losing my job," the shy little Cartugan girl confided to Denise the next day. "Mrs. Hendricks gave me a nice present to apologize, but I hope such a thing never happens again."

"I'm sure it won't," Denise said soothingly.

She wanted to ask Catalina whether there was any chance that she might have accidentally left the door unlocked after cleaning the suite, but could think of no tactful way of phrasing the question. Instead, she inquired about Luis Figueroa, whom she had met at the employees' Christmas party.

"Do you and Luis plan to be married soon?" she asked. "He seems like a nice boy — and a hard worker."

Catalina blushed proudly. "Luis takes care of all the hotel cars, and drives the guests into San Marco, or wherever they wish to go. He is not lazy like some *hombres* I know. But marriage —" She shrugged, and turned aside, but not before Denise had glimpsed a look of sorrow in the girl's lovely dark eyes. "We have spoken of this often," Catalina admitted. "Right now, though, it is impossible. First we must pay —"

"Yes?" Denise encouraged her.

Catalina bit her lip. An expression that might have been fear flickered across her face, but it was gone in a split-second. "A debt, that is all," she whispered. "First we must pay our debt."

This peculiar conversation lingered in Denise's mind long after the maid had left the room. She couldn't help wondering what sort of debt it was that Catalina and Luis had incurred. Credit cards and charge accounts were unknown in Cartuga's primitive economy. It really was none of her business, she told herself sternly. Nevertheless, she could not shake the conviction that Catalina was deeply troubled.

A few days later Vince Borden invited Denise,

Natalie, and Roger Gates to go along on what he termed a "working picnic."

"*Vacationland* magazine wants a full-color spread on the Caribe Azure for its next issue," he said. "They plan to stress the active sports angle. I thought we might use Tranquillity Isle for part of the lay-out."

"What a marvelous idea!" Denise enthused. From her seat in the lounge, the tiny islet a few hundred yards offshore looked more like a decoration on the gently rolling waters of the Caribbean than a real body of land. "I've often wanted to go over there and explore."

"Now's your chance," Vince grinned. "We'll head across right after breakfast tomorrow. Wear your bathing suit. I'll bring the cameras and have the chef pack us a lunch."

Natalie viewed the plan with misgivings. "It's quite a distance from shore," she murmured. "Have you a good strong boat that's guaranteed not to sink?"

Knowing her fear of the water, Vince tried to reassure her with a description of the hotel launch's inboard motor. "You'll love it, honey," he declared. "Besides, it will do you good to get away from these crowds of tourists for a day. Don't forget your golf clubs, Roger," he instructed. "The idea is to show that the Isle has everything the mainland resort has, only on a miniature scale."

Accordingly, after a smooth crossing that even Natalie seemed to enjoy, the group stepped out of the boat onto a fringe of creamy white beach. The entire islet was less than two acres in area but so cleverly planned and landscaped that none of the facilities seemed crowded. They roamed happily about for half an hour, until Vince became impatient to get the photography session underway.

"What *is* this place, anyway?" Denise asked, when finally they paused for lunch. "I mean, is it considered a separate island, or part of the Cartugan mainland, or what?"

" 'Or what,' I think," Vince laughed. "Technically, it's inside Cartuga's territorial waters. There are thousands of little rock outcroppings like this scattered along the coast. Ordinarily they're too barren to be of much use. When Senor Lorrimer bought the acreage for the hotel, he stipulated that this island be included in the purchase. He had tons of top-soil barged over here, and then transplanted trees and flowers and everything so that guests who wanted a day of seclusion could have it — in luxury. You know what a perfectionist he is. Nothing —"

"We know," Denise and Natalie chorused. "Nothing but the best for the Caribe Azure!"

"Right. During the slack season this summer, I believe he intends to have a cottage or two erected for the use of honeymooners," Vince added. "Meanwhile the beach, the little putting green and the tennis court offer privacy to anyone who wants to enjoy himself in solitary splendor."

Denise lay back on the warm sand, letting the foamy tide which scalloped the beach lap at her toes. The tiny island was like a miniature Garden of Eden. Occasionally, she found that the constant "togetherness" of resort hotel life got on her nerves. Here there was nothing but peace and quiet — and Vince's camera.

"Publicity, lovely publicity. Don't you ever get tired of focusing that lens?" Roger Gates lazily raised his driving iron and addressed the ball, holding the pose until the shutter had snapped.

"Never. We public relations men are absolutely tireless." Vince's jesting reply was made absent-mindedly. He jockeyed around, setting the shot up from another angle. "Think of all the sports addicts these photos will attract."

"I don't know about them, but I, for one, intend to spend all my days off over here, practicing my putting," Roger grinned. "This moss is pure green velvet."

Denise packed the remains of their lunch in the picnic basket while Vince posed Natalie beside the tennis net and reloaded his camera. She soon wandered back down to the beach, tired of watching. It had been a tedious morning. Vince was a relentless shutterbug, and her face ached from so many hours of "smiling for the birdie."

The water lured her in. Wading leisurely ahead, she found that the shallows extended forty or fifty feet out from the beach. Hardly a ripple marred the glassy surface. Peering down into the crystal depths, Denise was fascinated by the multitude of tiny sea creatures resting on the sandy bottom. No wonder scuba-diving was such a popular sport, she thought. If so much beauty existed here, this close to shore, what glorious sights the deeper waters must hold!

She toyed with the idea of renting an aqualung and trying it for herself. But the ambition was overruled by common sense. Even the most experienced frogmen seldom dived alone. Too many unexpected dangers could arise.

She splashed back up onto the beach. The photography session was still going on. "Vince, aren't you *ever* going to run out of film?" she demanded.

"Sure, pretty soon," he said vaguely. "Say, we've been trying to think up new gimmicks to coax the rich sportsmen over here from the neighboring islands. How does the idea of a wild boar hunt strike you? There are plenty of the beasts running loose in the mountains close by."

"In that case, I suggest you teach some of the natives how to hunt. They could probably use the food!"

As usual, the instant after she spoke Denise was regretting her rash outburst.

"Oh, I'm sorry, Vince," she apologized, scuffing at the sand. "I didn't mean to downgrade your suggestion. It's just that a lot of these people *are* going hungry. Once in a while the comparison between their way of life and — and all this leaves me feeling pretty ashamed."

"Hey, take it easy. Rome wasn't built in a day, you know," Vince said earnestly. "You'd be surprised at how much good is coming out of that glassy tower across the way."

"I'm sure you're right." Denise was too embarrassed to wish to stay and discuss the subject. "Look, you already have plenty of pictures of me. I'm going to swim back. You three can follow in the boat when you're ready."

Natalie sprang up in alarm. "Oh, don't! Something terrible might happen!"

"Heavens, it's less than half a mile. I could swim ten times that distance, if necessary." Denise yanked a cap over her dark hair, and dropped her sandals in the launch as she walked past it, pretending not to hear Vince's expostulations or Natalie's fearful warnings. Roger, at least, did not try to deter her. He was single-mindedly putting golf balls into a hole.

Denise slid into the calm, turquoise water, and struck out for the mainland. The swim was marvelously refreshing. Stroking briskly through the ripples she felt her frayed nerves relax, and her usual good humor come surging back. Here, in her favorite element, the feelings of resentment and frustration she had experienced on the island were washed away. Schools of fish darted back and forth far below her. She peered down, entranced by the greenish light which filtered through onto the white sand and coral. Thirty feet below lay a fascinating, wholly different world.

All too soon, however her feet touched bottom and she was wading along the foam-flecked expanse of sand which ringed the Caribe Azure's private beach. Several of the hotel's guests called a greeting to her as she strolled by, but she continued on with only a quick wave in their direction.

They were just people, she thought, still embarrassed by her earlier outburst. Rich — but people, nevertheless, most of them no different from her neighbors at home or the friends she had known all her life. It wasn't their fault that the islanders couldn't approach their standard of living. Martin Lorrimer and his public relations man were perfectly right in wanting to give them full value for the money they spent at the resort.

"Why," Denise groaned to herself, "do I always pick the wrong time to say the wrong thing?"

The droplets of water which clung to her shoulders and arms had already begun to evaporate in the strong afternoon sunshine by the time she had skirted the outdoor dining terrace and turned up the path leading to the employees' quarters. She paused for a moment to unsnap the close-fitting bathing cap; smoothing her hair back from her eyes, she glanced up and saw a tall young man striding diagonally across the pavilion toward her.

"Why, hello," John Westcott said, in what seemed to be genuine pleasure. "It's nice to see you again. As a matter of fact, I've just come from the pool. The boys there told me it was your day off." His grey eyes crinkled with amusement as they assessed her damp suit. "Busman's holiday?"

"In a way." Denise explained that she and the others had spent the morning over on the Isle. "Are you here on business?" she asked.

"No, actually I'm on my way to Santa Inez. Some friends of mine were married this morning. They invited me to join in the wedding celebration." His smile lost some of its self-assurance. "I wondered — I thought perhaps you might like to come with me. I would have telephoned you first, but until an hour ago I wasn't sure I could get away myself."

He was a young man who seemed to take his responsibilities very seriously, Denise thought. She guessed that he had little free time to spend on activities of a strictly social nature. She was complimented that he had chosen her to share in one of these occasions.

"Thank you, I'd like that very much," she accepted. "It won't take me long to change."

The prospects of this impromptu "date" left Denise with a more elated feeling than she had known in months. Since she had come to Cartuga the memory of Tim had faded deeper and deeper into the past. Now, suddenly, she found that she could think of him without the stab of pain which had once accompanied any remembrance of the way in which she had been jilted.

"I guess I'm not such a man-hater, after all," she admitted, discarding her bathing suit and stepping under the shower for a moment.

Tim, she realized now, hadn't been worth all the tears she had wasted on him. Nevertheless, she was determined to give her heart less hastily in the future. Somewhere, love was waiting for her — but she would walk, not run, to find it.

Ten minutes later, clad in a blue linen sheath dress which highlighted the brilliant hue of her eyes, and carrying a crisp white jacket and gloves, she emerged to find John waiting for her.

"I'm so glad you decided to ask me," she said, as he helped her into his jeep. "I've used several of my free days to travel around, trying to learn as much about Cartuga as I can. I have never been invited into an islander's home, though."

"That's probably because they are afraid of offending you," John explained. "Most of these people live quite humbly. They wouldn't expect an American girl to enjoy their simple way of life. Carlos and Maria are luckier than most," he added. "Quite a few tourists have chartered his boat for fishing trips this winter, so they will be starting their married life with a small nest egg for the future."

The town of Santa Inez lay about twenty miles up the coast. Denise's sightseeing jaunts had not yet carried her in this direction, so she took an interest in everything she saw. But John's remark about the newly-married couple reminded her of Catalina and Luis, and she soon found herself telling him about her friends at the hotel.

"I can't help feeling that they are involved in some sort of mystery," she said, in a voice that was faintly troubled. "Catalina looked downright scared when she mentioned the debt they owed. She and Luis are very much in love. I know they wouldn't keep on delaying their wedding unless something pretty formidable stood in their way." A sudden idea struck her. "Do you suppose they could have fallen into the clutches of some loan-shark?"

John kept his attention on the road until he had negotiated a sharp curve. "Could be. You'll find such people everywhere." He sounded a note of caution. "I wouldn't pry too much into their affairs. It sounds like a purely personal matter. Your friends might not appreciate having their secret exposed."

Denise realized that this was wise advice. She channeled the conversation onto another topic. "How is the water pipe project progressing?"

"All finished," he said proudly. "And the results have been nothing short of miraculous. The public health people report that recently in Soledad the spread of infectious diseases has been cut in half!"

"That *is* good to hear!" Denise couldn't help smiling at his enthusiastic tone. "Perhaps someday they'll have pure water facilities all over the island — thanks to you."

John shook his head. "Not me. I only gave them a hand. The government had already started the project. Since his election, Jorge Miras has done a tremendous job of improving living conditions here on Cartuga. It can't be done overnight, of course."

Denise nodded. Vince Borden, too, had reminded her that the old ways changed slowly. Too slowly, maybe — but they were changing.

Before she had time to ask any more questions, John applied the brakes and drove carefully through the outskirts of Santa Inez.

It was a small fishing village, set on the edge of a breathtakingly beautiful stretch of seacoast, with steep mountains rising directly behind the cluster of houses like a tropical green backdrop. There were no fences between the homes, and most of the yard space seemed to have been given over to the livestock. A pair of goats dozed in the shade provided by a rickety outbuilding, and chickens pecked and scratched listlessly at the hot, dusty ground.

Bright clumps of flowers and blossoming vines clinging to the houses made up for the lack of lawns and fresh paint, however, and Denise noticed that the boats moored on the beach looked well maintained.

The air was lively with the sound of music and a great deal of happy laughter. It was hard to keep from dancing as they alighted from the jeep and walked toward the house where the wedding was being celebrated. Balancing a bulky package under one arm, John took her elbow and steered her up the steps to the open-air veranda which ran the length of the house.

A sudden lull in the noise marked their entrance. Faces which had been open and smiling one moment abruptly changed to wary masks as soon as people caught sight of the strangers in their midst. The reaction eased, though, when Carlos, the young bridegroom, hurried across the room, clapped John on the shoulder, and introduced him to the throng with a burst of flowery Spanish. Denise, too, was welcomed as a friend. The last bit of constraint disappeared when John presented his gift to the bride. Maria immediately tore open the wrappings, and everyone in the room took turns admiring the shiny new set of copper-bottomed pots and pans.

"That must have been exactly the right thing to give," Denise complimented him later, when the music had resumed its pulsating beat, and the crowd had drifted back to the punchbowl and buffet table.

After sampling some of the refreshments, they escaped from the overflowing room onto the veranda, and tried a few dance steps to the rhythmic Latin strains. John held her lightly as they moved in time to the beat. Over his shoulder, Denise could see other couples swaying with more expert skill. The wedding guests seemed to be almost every color from creamy tan to deepest black, yet there was no consciousness of the different skin shades among the people.

She commented on this as they drove back to the hotel in the early evening twilight.

"Oh, integration isn't any problem here," John said. "Most of these islanders are of mixed blood. Nobody pays any attention to the color of a man's skin. Good thing, too — they've enough to combat without adding discrimination."

"Poverty, of course," Denise nodded. "But what else?"

"Communism is always a possibility in any developing country," John explained. "I don't think it will make many gains here, though. President Miras is seeing to it that people get decent housing and adequate salaries as quickly as possible. Then there's disease. The new public health program is coping with that. We're on our way to getting the problems licked."

He grinned ruefully. "All but the goofiest one, that is. The thing that really has everyone stumped is voodoo!"

Chapter Six

"Voodoo! Here? You're putting me on!"

John Westcott shook his head. His grin had vanished, and his expression was now completely serious.

"No, I'm not joking," he said. "Not about that stuff. We may be living in the space age, but nevertheless these hills are crawling with magic. Ask anyone. They'll tell you — if they dare."

Had his tone been less grim, Denise might have laughed. It sounded so utterly preposterous!

"But how can rational people believe all that hocus-pocus?" she demanded.

"It's part of their heritage." John's frown had intensified. "These islanders are terrifically superstitious, you know. They feel it would be tempting fate to break completely with the traditions of their ancestors. So even though the practice of voodoo, or obeah, as it's called on some of these islands, has been outlawed, the people still turn out in droves at the Friday night meetings to listen to the local *Houngan* or *Mambo*.

"To most of these high priests and priestesses, voodoo is a sort of religion, very ceremonial and relatively harmless." His knuckles tightened on the steering wheel. "But there are still a few around who practice *Wanga* — Black Magic. They specialize in spells, poison potions and evil charms. Believe me, it is no joking matter!"

In spite of herself, Denise could not repress a shiver. "Can't the police do anything about it?" she wondered.

"They've been trying, the last year or two. The old dictatorship tacitly encouraged the practice; voodoo, kept the people ignorant and docile," he explained. "The Miras government is doing what it can to make them close up shop, but the people won't cooperate — they're too darned scared to talk. What we need is proof positive that these witch doctors are phonies. That might open some eyes. Till then, I suppose voodoo will remain part of the culture."

"At least no one can say you lead a dull life," Denise dimpled. "Just think, you might have been posted somewhere very sedate and tame, like Edinburgh. Here, a rising young diplomat has unlimited advantages — drainage systems to build, magic spells to unbind —"

John laughed with her. "Yes, Cartuga is a challenge, and I love it." His grey eyes brushed her face. "My first year here has been downright hectic. Soon, though, I expect to have a bit more time to myself. I'm going back to the States on leave next week. After I return, I'd like to see you again."

"I'll be here," Denise murmured.

She was both sorry and glad to see the brightly-lit tower of the Caribe Azure winking ahead. Sorry, because the day spent in his company had been so pleasant; glad for the very reason that she *was* attracted to him. She had no intention of rushing her emotions for him or any man. Then, too, she realized that the girl who fell in love with John Westcott would also have to fall in love with his job, be willing to spend her life as he did, facing challenges in odd corners of the world.

She was not at all certain that that was what she wanted.

"Have a good vacation," she smiled, as he helped her alight from the jeep. "And thanks again for asking me along today. I enjoyed meeting your friends."

"Our first encounter without a misunderstanding," John added teasingly. "Good night, Denise."

It was nearly eight o'clock when they parted on the path leading to the employees' wing. After leaving her jacket and gloves in her room, Denise continued along to the dining hall, hoping to arrive before Natalie had finished eating. But the large room was nearly empty; rather than intrude on the conversations of the remaining few people whom she barely knew, she chose a small corner table near the kitchen and ordered a light meal.

She had just started on her dessert when a chair scraped nearby and she looked up to see Martin Lorrimer hovering over her.

"May I join you?" he asked. "No, please don't

get up. I wished to see you, and thought it might be more pleasant if we talked here."

A surprised waiter brought another cup of coffee to the table, then backed hastily through the kitchen door as though afraid he might drop something within the owner's earshot.

Denise, too, wondered at the purpose behind Senor Lorrimer's unaccustomed visit to this part of the hotel. It occurred to her that Vince Borden might have reported the incident which had occurred that morning on the Isle. With a sinking heart, she hoped that he had not pegged her as a trouble-maker.

But there was nothing in his attitude to indicate that this was the case. Looking as dapper and unperturbed as ever, he chatted politely about the weather until she had finished her fruit compote. Only then did he broach the subject which concerned him.

"As you know, I try to make sure that everyone in my hotel is content," he said. "That includes the people who work here, as well as the guests. I think we are reasonably successful in that aim, but it is best to be certain. Tell me, are you happy here, Miss O'Shea?"

She nodded. "Yes, I am. Very. This is a beautiful place to work and live, Senor Lorrimer." Lowering her eyelids, she took a deep breath. Might as well face the music. "I've already apologized to Vince Borden for my remarks this morning. I hadn't realized he would consider what I said important enough to bring to your attention."

"Ah, but it could be important, though perhaps not in the way you believe." He spread his arms wide in a gesture of appeal. "For some time now, certain government officials and I have been discussing a plan. But before I describe it to you, I would like to know what prompted your anger today. Someone new to the island often sees things differently from we who have spent our whole lives here. Your reactions might make the perspective clearer for me."

He was so obviously sincere that Denise felt a rush of relief. He wasn't angry — just puzzled. And maybe Vince's tale-bearing hadn't been malicious, after all!

She took her time, trying to describe honestly and without prejudice the distress she invariably felt whenever she considered the disparity between the luxury of life at the Caribe Azure, and the poverty-stricken existence of the majority of the islanders.

"Truly, I didn't mean to criticize the hotel," she assured him. "I heard President Miras say that because of their jobs here many people will have a better life. And, of course, every tourist who comes spends money at the markets and shops, so this helps the economy, too. I know it takes time — even John Westcott told me not to expect miracles overnight."

Martin Lorrimer was leaning forward, listening intently to every word. "I see you have given this problem a great deal of thought," he observed. "Had it occurred to you that there might be some way in which you, yourself, could help?"

Ruefully, Denise shook her head. "I'm afraid it hadn't." The admission made her feel ashamed. She glanced sheepishly at him. "I'm a fine one to talk, aren't I? But I really would like to help."

"I was hoping you would say that," the hotel owner smiled. "I am sure your assistance will prove valuable. You see, we want to start a physical fitness program for the children of San Marco."

Whatever "plan" Denise had expected to hear about, it certainly was not this. "You mean — exercise?" she faltered. "Running and jumping, and —"

"— and swimming. Exactly. You are surprised?"

"Truthfully, yes," she confessed. "I know that keeping fit is important, but I would have thought that schools and housing and better food would come first."

"Much has already been done along those lines," he assured her. "But President Miras, as well as the President of your own great country, feels that to fully enjoy these benefits our young citizens must be kept strong and healthy.

"The government has set aside a large strip of land just outside the capital for use as a park," he continued. "The facilities include a baseball field, tennis courts, and a public swimming pool.

We have even arranged for buses to transport the school children back and forth. Now all we need are qualified instructors who are willing to spend a few hours a week getting the program underway."

"And you want me to teach the children to swim? I'd love to!" Denise's eyes sparkled with anticipation. "I'm sure Natalie Engstromm will volunteer, too, the minute she hears about the need." As they rose to leave the dining room, another question occurred to her. "The money for the equipment — it's coming from the hotel, isn't it?"

"Yes, but that fact must remain our secret. It is better if the park be considered a gift from the government of Cartuga to its people," Martin Lorrimer insisted.

Beneath the smooth moustache, his small white teeth gleamed in a brief smile. "Actually, this whole idea was my mother's. She is a very determined lady. She approached President Miras about the program personally, then badgered me to supply the funds." He shrugged philosophically. "It is little enough I can do to keep her happy. Since my sister's death she has had few interests."

After parting from her boss, Denise went in search of Natalie. She found her blonde friend with Vince Borden in the recreation room.

Vince grinned good-naturedly at her when she had finished telling Natalie about the physical fitness program.

"Now, aren't you sorry you yelled at me this morning?" he teased. "I was all for recruiting you girls weeks ago, but the boss wouldn't let me ask you until I'd convinced him you would really be interested. He hates imposing on others, even though he himself spends half his time serving on public committees."

"Senor Lorrimer mentioned that his mother was the guiding force behind this new plan," Denise remarked. "It seems odd that I've never met her."

"I know the reason for that," Natalie confided. "Mama Elena told me that Senora Lorrimer refuses to live here at the hotel. Nothing her son says can persuade her to leave her friends in the old mountain town of Dos Rios. I understand she does a great deal of charity work."

"Yes, and the alms she distributes come from the Caribe Azure," Vince chuckled. "Senor Lorrimer doesn't really mind, though. To a Latin, family is all-important. Anything a relative desires is his without question."

From him the girls learned that the new park was nearing completion. Within two or three weeks, he said, the physical fitness program should be getting underway. He also added that a number of other volunteers had come forward, offering to help coach the youngsters, so the work could be divided without placing a burden on anyone.

Oddly enough, Denise's regular job responsibilities seemed to be dwindling. During the next few days, she became aware of a definite decline in the hotel's population. Most of the "jet-setters" had, at least temporarily, abandoned the Caribe Azure, flying off to Acapulco and Rio and other, gayer, winter resorts. She thought little of this, since the international group tended to fluctuate a great deal, anyway. But when even the staid, semi-permanent residents of the hotel began departing in cliques of threes and fours, she asked Martin Lorrimer the reason behind their exodus.

"It is because of Mardi Gras," he sighed. "Here in Cartuga we seem to slip into Lent almost without noticing it, but elsewhere in Latin America Carnival time is a season of great revelry. In a week or ten days most of our guests will return.

"As a matter of fact," he added, "this lull might be a good time for some of the staff to take a little vacation. If you desire to have a few days off, this can easily be arranged."

"You honestly wouldn't mind?" A tingle of excitement stirred within Denise. "I *would* love to see a Mardi Gras parade!"

"The spectacle is well worth witnessing. Perhaps Miss Engstromm would like to accompany you," Senor Lorrimer suggested. "Your only difficulty would lie in securing room reservations. Jamaica and San Juan will be impossibly crowded. But if you were thinking of going to Haiti, I could ask my hotel in Port-Au-Prince to hold space for you."

Denise was touched by his generosity and thoughtfulness. "You are much too kind to us," she smiled. "May I discuss this with Natalie and let you know tonight? I'm sure she will be every bit as thrilled as I am."

It was all she could do to keep from running as she crossed the pavilion and entered the tennis court enclosure. To her relief, she found that Natalie had finished giving her last lesson of the day, and was practicing a few backhand serves with Vince Borden as a partner.

"Stop being so energetic and come sit down," Denise called. "I've got some wonderful news. How would you like to go to Haiti?"

"Haiti?" Natalie's pert little face looked blank. "Whatever for?"

"Mardi Gras!" Denise squealed. "Senor Lorrimer has offered to limp along without our services for a few days, since so many of the guests will be away. He can even wangle hotel rooms for us in Port-Au-Prince! Doesn't it sound marvelous? Exotic costumes, dancing and singing in the streets —"

"Heavens, you're acting like an animated ad for American Express!" Natalie giggled, and glanced up at Vince, who was still mopping his brow from the strenuous exertion. "It really would be fun, though. Could you get time off, too? With all that holiday revelry going on, I'd feel safer with a big, strong escort."

Vince hooted in derision. "Honey, with all

your energy, you could run any man ragged in an hour! But seriously, I do think it would be best if you two nitwits had a keeper in tow. Possibly even a pair of them, so I wouldn't have to dance with both of you at once. How about inviting Roger Gates to go along?"

"We could," Denise consented, somewhat reluctantly. Except for the "working picnic" and a few casual encounters, she had seen little of Roger since their pre-Christmas shopping excursion. "Do you suppose he would be interested? He keeps to himself a great deal when he isn't out on the golf course."

"I think he's just lonely. A holiday away from his five-iron will do him good," Vince declared. He picked up his racquet, and slung his sweater across his shoulders. "I'll check with Roger, then see about airline reservations. What say we plan on leaving Monday morning, and return on Wednesday?"

The girls agreed to this schedule, deciding that it would give them time enough to enjoy the festivities as well as some leeway for sightseeing in Port-Au-Prince. The Carnival celebration lasted an entire week, but the culmination would come on Tuesday, the day before Ash Wednesday, so they would arrive in time for the most important events.

Shortly after they had returned to their rooms, Vince telephoned to say that Roger had been delighted at the invitation to join the group. Luckily, the public relations man had succeeded in reserving the last four seats available on any plane leaving Cartuga for Haiti on Monday.

The days before their departure seemed to pass very slowly; once airborne, however, the minutes flew by with astonishing speed. In less than an hour they had landed outside Haiti's capital city. The drive into Port-Au-Prince was a fascinating adventure. The streets were jammed with both automobiles and burros, neither of which seemed to obey any particular set of traffic signals.

Gazing excitedly out the window, Denise spotted beautiful modern buildings standing side-by-side with primitive huts, and Natalie pointed out a number of houses which appeared to have been erected on stilts. Haiti's first city was like no other capital in the world!

"Gosh, and I thought Cartuga was a colorful place," Vince exclaimed, eyeing the peasant women who walked with grace and dignity while balancing enormous baskets of fruits and vegetables on their heads.

Roger bobbed his red-brown head in enthusiastic agreement. "No wonder the Caribe Azure is all but deserted!"

All business seemed to have been suspended in the downtown portion of the harbor city. Their driver was forced to take a roundabout route to avoid the merrymakers who thronged the streets. Above the tumult and laughter of the crowds, an incessant drum beat throbbed and pounded. Denise's blood raced faster in her veins. Nearly everyone she glimpsed was masked, some in comic paper-mache headgear, others in enveloping hoods which looked terrifyingly fierce.

Not even the foot-thick walls of the hotel could totally muffle the outside din, but the girls' room at the end of a sixth-floor corridor was relatively quiet so long as the shutters were kept tightly closed. It was also unbearably hot.

"Oh, well," laughed Natalie, throwing open a window. "I don't suppose anyone bothers much about sleep at a time like this. From the looks of those revelers, they keep going until they drop, then start up again after a short nap on the pavement!"

Denise dropped down on one of the twin beds to glance through a pamphlet describing local points of interest.

"Too bad, we haven't time to visit Cape Haitien and see the Citadelle and Sans Souci Palace," she lamented. "But perhaps the fellows will take us out to browse through the Iron Market."

Natalie peered over her shoulder. "Sounds like a two-square-block junk market to me," she retorted dubiously. "The souvenir shops are my weakness. My Cousin Sally would love one of those tortoise-shell ornaments. Look, it says you can even buy authentic voodoo trophies!"

Denise's pulse quickened. There was that word again. Voodoo! Apparently, the cult of spells and incantations was much stronger here than on Cartuga. The pamphlet made the ritualistic dances sound eerily fascinating.

She reminded herself that their time in Haiti was tightly limited, and that the main purpose of their visit was to watch the Mardi Gras festivities. Even so, her curiosity about the practice which John Westcott found so repugnant was beginning to grow.

But before she could more than acknowledge this to herself, it was time to join Vince and Roger for lunch. From then until Wednesday morning, it seemed that there was hardly a minute free for breathing.

In the afternoons, the foursome explored Port-Au-Prince by bus and on foot; in the evenings they mingled with the sidewalk crowds viewing the pageantry on the streets. On Tuesday night, in hastily assembled costumes of their own, they attended a masked ball. By Ash Wednesday, even indefatigable Natalie admitted to exhaustion.

"But we still haven't bought any souvenirs," she complained that morning, after a late breakfast. "Have we time for an hour's shopping, Vince? My family would never forgive me if I didn't send them some little trinket from Haiti."

"You and your relatives!" he exclaimed, shaking his head indulgently. "All right — but just an hour. What direction shall we take?"

"Down this way. I saw some terrific buys in sisal —" The little blonde hurried off, tugging Vince along behind her.

With Roger's ailing back in mind, Denise set a more leisurely pace. She had already bought a hand-polished mahogany bowl for her parents from the hotel's gift shop, and so was more interested in observing the Haitian people than in making any special purchases.

"I've been trying to get my ear attuned to the language they speak here," she said. "It sounds like French, but it isn't, quite."

"It's a sort of a Creole dialect," he told her. "You often hear the same sort of patois in the old quarters of New Orleans."

He was limping more noticeably now, and Denise feared that the constant activity of the past two days might have aggravated his old injury. To give him a chance to rest, she slowed to a stroll and lingered in front of the shop windows. A number of the stores still had a deserted look to them. She suspected that their proprietors were home in bed, recovering from an overdose of Carnival gaiety.

Glancing down the block, she noted that her other friends had momentarily disappeared. "Here are some of the tortoise-shell combs Natalie was admiring," she remarked, moving on to the next window. "I wonder if she saw this display."

"It wouldn't have done her much good," Roger pointed out. "They don't seem to be open for business." He looked at his watch, and started to take her arm. "We ought to be getting back. Our flight —"

Denise's startled gasp interrupted him. She pressed closer to the window, straining for a better view of the sparkling bauble which commanded her attention.

"Roger, that looks like — I'm sure it is! Mrs. Hendricks' necklace!"

"What!" He moved forward, dubiously eyeing the glittering display. "That's just costume jewelry," he laughed. "Her collection of sparklers must have cost thousands of dollars."

"They did. But it's the same necklace. I'm positive!"

But even as she voiced the opinion, Denise's common sense asserted itself. What business would real emeralds and rubies have in a window crowded with native handicraft?

"I wish I could see the price tag," she grumbled. "That would soon settle my doubts."

This time there was a hint of impatience in Roger's tone. "I wish you could, too. But short of breaking the window, I'm afraid you're doomed to disappointment. And, as I started to mention, our flight leaves at 1:55 sharp!"

Plain logic warned Denise that he was right. Still, she hesitated. That particular glass case was filled almost to overflowing with tortoise-shell jewelry, carved mahogany figurines and cleverly woven sisal handbags. On a higher shelf, exotic looking *rada* drums and shriveled amulets were offered for sale.

Voodoo trophies!

Behind her, Natalie's excited chatter and

Vince's voice blended with Roger's warning tones. Denise darted a final look at the necklace in the window. For a reason she could not quite explain, she made a careful mental note of the shop's name and street address. Then she was being hustled along, back to the hotel to collect the luggage and on to the airport with only minutes to spare.

Once aboard the plane, Roger sank into an aisle seat and closed his eyes. It had been an enjoyable holiday, but tiring, and as soon as Natalie and Vince had stowed the bags of souvenirs in the overhead luggage compartment, they, too, leaned back to doze.

Only Denise remained upright, wide-eyed despite her fatigue. *Had* it been Myra Hendricks' necklace back there in the window? She couldn't put the memory of its brilliant beauty out of her mind. And if it were not, she frowned, even if it were no more than a paste imitation, how had an exact duplicate come to be in such an unexpected spot?

A twinge of uneasiness skittered up her spine. "Right below the voodoo trophies!" she whispered to herself.

Chapter Seven

Gradually, the smooth flight back to Cartuga and the contagious air of drowsiness within the plane lulled away Denise's distress.

"I must have been imagining things," she yawned to herself, as she prepared to leave the aircraft.

During the past hour, she had become more and more convinced that the gems displayed among the hodgepodge of goods in the shop window were but a gaudy imitation of the genuine jewels owned by Mrs. Hendricks. She felt a trifle foolish at having jumped to such a rash conclusion, and hoped that Roger would refrain from mentioning the incident to anyone.

Luckily, he appeared to have already forgotten about the embarrassing scene.

"I haven't had such a good time in years," he said, assisting Denise out of the car that had transported them from the airport to the Caribe Azure. He included all of them in his smile. "Thanks for asking me along."

"Glad you could come." Vince toted Natalie's assortment of souvenirs as far as the entrance to the womens' quarters, and set them inside with an air of relief. "Tip the Redcap, lady?"

"Sorry, but I'm fresh out of pesos — or

gourdes, as they say in Haiti." Natalie wrinkled her nose at him. "But even though I'm penniless, it was a Mardi Gras I'll never forget!"

"Neither will I — if I ever wake up." Denise muffled another yawn. "You're a marvelous escort, Vince. I'll see you both after I've had a day or two of siesta."

A few hours' sleep was plenty to refresh her, however. After a brisk shower, she joined Catalina and Mama Elena for dinner. Since neither of them had ever ventured beyond the shores of their own island, she described the Carnival in detail for them.

Recounting her experiences in Port-Au-Prince reminded her once again of the morning's peculiar mix-up. There really was no cause for alarm, she told herself insistently. Yet a last, shadowy doubt still remained. To silence it once and for all, she excused herself after dinner and strolled across the terrace to the guests' outdoor dining area.

Myra Hendricks waved and called to her as she threaded her way among the tables. Denise answered with a smile of pleasure. One glance at the lustrous circle of gems adorning Mrs. Hendricks' throat had banished her last trace of uncertainty. The necklace was still here in Cartuga, safely in its owner's possession!

"It's so nice to see you back," the older woman exclaimed. "Did you have a good vacation?"

"It was frantic, but fun," Denise replied.

"Haiti is a fascinating country. Have you ever been there?"

"No, Walter has never cared much for traveling. Perhaps we will take a long trip together, one of these days."

Denise let the subject drop, determined to forget the episode in Port-Au-Prince. Obviously, her imagination had been working overtime!

She settled back in her chair, but the flashing stones across the table caught and held her eye. Imagination or not, there really was an amazing similarity between the two pieces of jewelry!

The following week, several busloads of Cartugan school children were shepherded down the paths of the new park, divided into classes, and started on their way toward physical fitness.

At first, some of the younger ones hung shyly back, refusing to go near the water. Denise felt her own timidity vanishing as she tried to help them overcome their fears. There was an appealing sweetness about the wide-eyed youngsters, yet an impish grin flashing here and there reassured her that they were no different from children anywhere.

Although they listened politely, a few giggles at her American accent greeted her first attempt to speak to them. Denise promptly grinned back at the teasers, and chose the most mischievous-looking boy to help demonstrate the beginning lesson. He cooperated eagerly when he found that he could safely touch bottom. Before long, the whole group of children was holding onto the bar at the shallow end of the pool, kicking and splashing with gleeful determination.

Fleet-footed Natalie was given the task of organizing relay races, while two former baseball stars set about teaching a group of boys the rudiments of softball. Other instructors scrambled about on the monkey bars, setting the pace for "follow the leader." Formal calisthenics would come later; the idea now was to get the children interested in exercise for the fun of it.

Denise rode back to the hotel tired but happy after having given half-hour lessons to four separate classes. In the seat next to her, Natalie rubbed her aching legs and groaned that she had done enough running that day to equal ten sets of singles at Forest Hills.

"I'll be glad when those kids develop enough coordination to learn tennis," she sighed.

Both girls had agreed to work with the children three afternoons a week. At first this schedule seemed rather formidable when combined with their regular duties, but it wasn't long before Denise declared that she found the job more rewarding and stimulating than merely sitting by the Caribe Azure's pool to ward off emergencies.

By the end of the second week her young pupils were showing definite signs of progress. They displayed even more eagerness to learn when some of their parents began visiting the park to watch them perform. Denise became so accustomed to adults filling the benches at poolside that until she had finished giving her last lesson of the day she failed to notice that one of the spectators seemed to have eyes for her alone.

When the children had scampered off to shower and change, John Westcott ambled over and extended a hand to help her out of the pool.

"Welcome back!" she greeted him, noticing that in his casual sports clothes he looked bronzer and more bursting with energy than ever. "But must you *always* catch me when I'm soaking wet?"

His grey eyes crinkled. "Well, considering your profession —"

"You have a point there. Nowadays, it seems I hardly dry out from morning to night," Denise confessed. She spread the towel out on the bench and sat down, more pleased to see him than she would have thought possible. "You look as if your leave agreed with you. Did you spend the whole time sunbathing in Florida?"

"Nope — skiing in Colorado. Family reunion," John said. "I'd forgotten what a shock it is to change climates so quickly. I still haven't regained my 'island legs' as yet."

Denise laughed. "A few more days of Cartuga's heat will take care of that."

"I was hoping that you would help the process along, by letting me take you dancing tomorrow night."

He explained that he had only arrived back

that noon, and was obliged to report in at the Consulate.

"But barring earthquakes or a declaration of war, I still have two days left of my vacation," he added. "If I don't keep you out too late Saturday evening, perhaps you'd like to spend Sunday with me, as well. There's a special spot I want to show you."

Denise laughed up at him. "Now you've aroused my curiosity! I'd love to go dancing, John. And I am scheduled to be off on Sunday. I suppose we may as well make the most of your last free day, before you get involved with another drainage ditch, or something."

His smiling eyes seemed to promise that no project, however important, would keep him from seeing her as often as possible. He helped her on with her terrycloth jacket, and walked with her to where the car waited.

"See you tomorrow. Eight o'clock," he said.

Under Luis's expert handling, the big sedan sped smoothly back to the Caribe Azure. After fending off a question or two from Natalie, Denise leaned against the seat cushions and tried to marshal her thoughts. This was only the fourth time she had seen John Westcott, yet she could no longer avoid the conviction that she was falling in love with him. Everything about the serious young diplomat, from his inclination to put duty first to his evident affection for the Cartugan people, attracted her. He was so entirely different from Tim!

Nevertheless, she battled against the upsurge of emotion that the pressure of his hand on hers had created. Her heart, cleared of the debris from her old, broken romance, was ready and waiting for someone to love. Still, intuition warned her to wait before bestowing her affections a second time.

Since coming to Cartuga, Denise had had no lack of opportunity for meeting presentable young men. Good-looking hotel guests frequently invited her out for a whirl at San Marco's night life, and she occasionally accepted one of these invitations. But until meeting John Westcott, she had encountered no one who had won her whole-hearted respect and admiration.

Even so, she reminded herself that in reality she knew very little about him. Perhaps it was just as well that for the next few months her loyalties must remain with the Caribe Azure. The terms of her contract would act as an impediment to haste, keep her from rushing into anything which she might later regret.

Promptly at eight o'clock the next evening, John escorted her to a car which he had borrowed for the occasion. "My jeep is not nearly grand enough to convey you to the ball, Cinderella," he stated gallantly.

"Dear me! And I thought the Latin Americans had cornered the market on chivalrous flattery." Denise noticed that he, himself, looked undeniably handsome in his white dinner jacket.

"Thank you, Prince Charming!"

During the ride in to the city, she led the conversation around to his home life. John enthusiastically described the members of his large family.

"I went back mainly to act as godfather to my youngest nephew," he added. "Also, I wanted to reassure my folks that I hadn't come down with malaria or anything from living in the tropics. Mother and Dad can't understand anyone voluntarily leaving Colorado. Living in that valley surrounded by mountains is their idea of heaven."

"But not yours?"

"Yes, mine too," John admitted. "That's one reason I entered the diplomatic service. I knew that not very many people in this world had a chance at a life like that. It might sound foolish, but I hoped I could help even things up a bit."

Later, as they moved across the dance floor to the strains of a haunting Latin melody, he told Denise that he had thought about her a great many times while he was away. "I couldn't wait to get back and see you again."

"I was wondering how you knew where to find me yesterday," she confessed.

John grinned. "That's where a good intelligence service comes in handy. To be truthful, Martin Lorrimer told me. He was seeing someone off at the airport when my plane came in, and offered me a lift back to town. He seems very proud that you girls are taking such an interest in his pet project."

"It's certainly no great chore," Denise laughed. "They are so eager to learn that it's a real pleasure teaching them."

As they drove back to the hotel through the balmy March air, she asked if he intended to keep his plans for the next day a secret.

John nodded. "Wear a bathing suit under your skirt and blouse," he advised. "And don't eat too large a breakfast. All else must remain shrouded in mystery."

From these tantalizing hints, Denise surmised that his plans included swimming. More than once before falling asleep that night, she wondered what the next day held in store. Whatever it was, she decided at last, in John's company it could not help but prove enjoyable.

By eleven o'clock the following morning the sturdy jeep was jouncing along the coast road in the direction of Santa Inez. Denise turned several times to peer at the peculiarly-shaped lumps on the back seat, but John refused to let her so much as peek beneath the blankets which concealed the objects, insisting that this would spoil the surprise.

This time they bypassed the village without stopping, and continued on with only the vivid mountain backdrop and the crisp sea breeze for company. In places the churning surf had eroded the shoreline, nibbling away at the land until only a yard or so of earth separated the increasingly bumpy road from the water. Along other stretches, jagged outcroppings of rock alternated with patches of sand. But not until they had rounded a point and pulled off on the edge of the road did Denise have any clue to their destination.

Ahead and just below them, shimmering in the sunlight, lay the most beautiful golden crescent of beach she had ever seen. A long, sloping sandbar reached far out into the sea at the upper end of the curve, protecting the rim of sand from the pounding waves and forming a natural harbor. Framed by lush tropical trees, and with gulls circling lazily overhead, it looked to Denise like some movie mogul's dream of an island Paradise come true. In Technicolor!

"Oh, John, how perfectly lovely!" she cried. "This is your surprise? It's perfect!"

"There's more," he informed her, hopping out and burrowing in the back seat. "We're going to dive for treasure!"

"What!"

She watched in amazement as he hauled a pair of aqua-lung tanks from beneath the blankets. Soon, flippers, goggles and a spear-gun were added to the pile of equipment.

"See that lagoon?" he pointed, obviously delighted at her astonishment. "Carlos showed it to me one day. The bones of an old Spanish galleon are buried down there. A pirate ship, legend has it, that blew ashore during a storm and sank in this very spot!"

Excitedly, Denise scooped up an armload of

gear and carried it down the slope to the water's edge while John followed with the rest of the equipment.

"You must be a mind-reader!" she exclaimed. "I've been dying to learn to scuba-dive. But there was never anyone to go with me, and I was a little afraid to try it alone."

"That's only common sense," John said, matter-of-factly. "You never know what you might encounter down below. There shouldn't be any sharks in this vicinity, but I've brought along a spear-gun just in case anything should show signs of attacking."

He helped fasten the tank of air to her back, and showed her how the breathing apparatus worked. "These heavy rubber flippers should protect our feet from coral cuts," he added, tugging on his own pair. "And since it's only three or four fathoms deep, we should have no problem with the bends. All you have to do is keep your eyes open and follow me."

Denise peered out at the frothing wavelets. "Do you really think there's treasure down there?"

"Probably not," John grinned, "although the galleon is reputed to have sunk sometime during the 1540's when shipments of gold were being pirated all over the Caribbean. But I've been wanting to go down and take a look ever since Carlos showed me the spot. With luck, we might even bring up an ancient doubloon or two!"

She found it awkward to walk with the cumbersome flippers strapped to her feet, but by moving slowly she managed to follow John around to the center of the sandbar. Here he lowered himself into the crystal-clear water, and beckoned for her to do the same.

Once immersed, Denise found the flippers to be an asset rather than the hindrance they had been on shore. The heavy air tank, too, had a surprising buoyancy. She all but floated to the center of the lagoon. On the surface the sea was sunlight-warm, and the lapping waves caressed her skin.

But John gave her no time to linger. When he judged that they had swum the proper distance, he jackknifed below the surface. Within seconds, only a trail of bubbles mingled with the gently lapping waves to mark the spot where he had submerged.

Denise ducked under the water in pursuit. A few strong kicks propelled her downward. Through the large goggles she had no trouble keeping him in sight, and she stared avidly around while descending. Schools of darting, rainbow-hued fish skittered aside at her approach, only to resume formation when she had passed. Apparently, they regarded her and John as some strange sea creatures!

Gradually the environment darkened as the tons of water overhead blotted out much of the sun's light. It was much cooler, now. In the weird half-light of this undersea world everything began to look shadowy and neutral in color. When she spotted columns of marine plants stretching toward the surface, Denise guessed that they must be nearing the ocean floor.

Half a minute later, her foot touched bottom. John snapped on the underwater flashlight he had brought along. By its slender beam, Denise glimpsed a few shells littering the sand, and noticed some odd coral formations which she took care to avoid. An unearthly stillness reigned at the bottom of the lagoon. Here there was no lapping of waves, no shriek of birds or whisper of wind to break the silence.

John touched her arm, pointing to the left. Moving in what seemed like slow-motion, they forged ahead. Now and then a dark shape slithered across the sand, leaving tiny whirlpools of disturbance in its wake.

Denise had no way of gauging the time which had elapsed. She had almost become convinced that they were heading in the wrong direction when suddenly a form, wavery enough to be thought a mirage, loomed up before her eyes. It took substance as they drew nearer, and her startled gaze identified the hull of a once-proud sailing ship!

She and John clasped hands in triumph. They had found the pirate galleon!

The great beams of the vessel had split open, leaving a hundred exits and entrances ajar for anyone daring enough to use them. John's light searched the battered old hulk. It illuminated nothing except rotted timbers and centuries of rust encrusting the iron fittings.

Single-file, they entered the wreck.

"Davy Jones' Locker," Denise thought, shivering when she remembered the doom which had befallen the men who had sailed this ship. She fervently hoped they would encounter no skeletons!

A big fish, startled by the unaccustomed light, darted frantically away. Denise jumped as it streaked past her, and took a step or two backward when a baby octopus scuttled through another gaping hole. With the departure of these former occupants, they appeared to have the derelict to themselves, however, and soon she was keeping pace with John, exploring every inch of bulkhead and deck space which had not long since been reduced to pulp by the relentless sea.

They came upon a pair of cannon, now so rusted that they were barely recognizable. Splintery holes in the remaining planks showed where they had crashed through the upper decks when the timbers weakened and gave way. But aside from these relics of buccaneering days, there was little else of interest to be found.

Finally, with a motion toward his air tank gauge, John signaled that their oxygen supply was decreasing past the safety level. He guided her through one of the splits in the hull, and swam protectively close behind her as they paddled upward.

Denise was not at all sorry to break through to the surface of the lagoon. Her very bones felt chilled by the hour spent in "Davy Jones' Locker." The sun on her shoulders was luxuriously warm, and it was a relief to rip away the face mask and draw fresh, pure air into her lungs once again.

"Disappointed?" John asked, when they had floundered up onto the beach and discarded their diving gear.

"Heavens, no!" Denise laughed. "It was a marvelous adventure. I hadn't really expected to discover any pirate gold, had you?"

He shook his head. "Anything remaining after all these years must be covered by a ton of sand. But it was fun to look."

Denise toweled her hair dry, then stretched out and let the hot sun evaporate the moisture from the trim, one-piece bathing suit. In a surprisingly short time, when John tactfully returned to the jeep for a few minutes, she was able to pull on her skirt and blouse and replenish her lipstick.

When he returned, dressed in khaki slacks and a sports shirt, he suggested that they share an early dinner.

"I've heard of a little restaurant not far from here which is supposed to be good but not fancy," he said. "The cooking is strictly native-style. Feel like trying it?"

"Indeed I do," Denise agreed enthusiastically. "This fresh air seems to be influencing my appetite. Or maybe it was the sight of all those fish down there — dinner on the fin, you might say!"

A few miles farther up the coast road, they entered what appeared to be a thriving fishing community. The market place was deserted this late in the day, but the cafe adjacent to the wharf was open for business and already boasted quite a number of patrons.

While they were being escorted to a small, gaily decorated table near the window, Denise experienced a queer, prickly sensation. Explorers in the jungle, she thought, might have felt the same inner warning, as though hostile eyes were following their every move. But most of the people looked friendly, if a trifle curious, and she was far too hungry to let apprehension spoil what had so far been a perfect day.

Almost before she had time to glance around, a large, steaming tureen was placed on the table. The waiter deftly ladled a thick, savory-smelling chowder into their bowls, then returned with a basket heaping with crisp rolls and tall glasses of iced tea.

The soup proved to be a kind of seafood stew, similar to the Spanish *paella*. Shrimp, scallops, clams and oysters, as well as bits of sausage and unidentifiable fish, were combined in the hearty dish. Denise finished her second bowlful with a sigh of satisfaction, then declared that never before had she been served anything so simple in appearance which tasted so delicious.

"I think Senor Lorrimer is missing a bet, not

featuring this on the hotel menu," she told John. "Why, the Americans —"

"Americans, pah!"

Denise jumped six inches. She and John had been so engrossed with their dinner and with each other that neither of them had noticed the gigantic youth who had crossed the room and now stood, arms akimbo, glaring down at them.

"Americans are not welcome in Cartuga," he continued in a venomous tone. His gaze fastened on John. "Especially those of your sort. Always preaching, cajoling the people. Telling them what they should or should not do. It would be much safer for the Americans if they went back where they came from!"

Denise was both frightened and baffled by this unprovoked tirade. Her eyes darted toward the other diners, but they could hardly be classed as allies. Every single person was studiously staring in the opposite direction, even though the haughty, strangely accented voice boomed out loudly enough to reach the farthest corners of the room.

Calmly, John laid aside his napkin and pushed back his chair. Tall as he was, the young giant towered above him. If it came to a fight, Denise thought desperately, the other man had the advantage of both height and weight!

But John chose to answer the challenge with words, rather than fists.

"You cannot speak for the people of Cartuga, Orestes, since you are not one of them," he retorted. "Jorge Miras himself preaches against ignorance and superstition. Perhaps it is you who should return to where you came from!"

"We will see who leaves first."

The boastful threat was accompanied by a glare of pure hatred. For a full minute, the eyes of the two men remained locked in silent combat. Then Orestes spun on his heel and stalked from the room.

"Wh-what was all that about?" Denise stammered.

With a visible effort, John relaxed. "You might say it's a business matter," he replied, trying to grin but without a great deal of success. "He blames me for driving away some of his mother's customers. She's one of the *mambos* I told you about — the sort who mixes black magic with her voodoo!"

Chapter Eight

John waited until they were safely back in the jeep before telling her the rest of the story.

"Orestes Tigue and his mother came over here from Haiti a few years back," he said. "She was a very powerful and well-known *mambo* there, but when rumors began circulating that her spells had resulted in someone's death, the police were obliged to step in. The Tigue family escaped to Cartuga, however, and apparently the Haitian authorities were so relieved to be rid of them that they never bothered with extradition."

"And now she's doing the same sort of thing here?" Denise asked. "It's strange that the Cartugan people would accept a foreigner as head of their cult."

John explained that the *mambo*'s reputation was quite widespread. "Curiosity mixed with superstition brought the followers to her *hounfor*, or voodoo temple, but I suspect that terror and blackmail have cemented her hold over the people. I've talked to half a dozen natives who attend the ceremonies. All of them are scared stiff of her *Wanga* — black magic."

"Even so, you must be making some progress. Otherwise Orestes wouldn't resent your interference so much," Denise encouraged him.

John continued to grumble but his expression softened as they approached the lagoon. The barely rippling waters of the cove had, like a vast, swaying prism, captured the sunset's ebbing glory. A rainbow of jewel tones sparkled on its placid surface.

"It would be a shame to let that fellow spoil our day," he said. "Let's forget all about him, and instead talk about our next outing together. I'll be on duty this coming weekend. My time is my own for the one after that, though."

"Then you can join us for the fiesta!" Denise cried. "Senor Lorrimer is planning an all-day gala to celebrate Cartuga's Independence Day on April 3rd. From what I've heard, it should be like Mardi Gras and the Fourth of July rolled into one!"

"Roman candles and limbo dancers, huh? Sounds like the best party of the year." A smile creased his tanned face, making it look boyishly carefree. "Still, I'd much rather have you all to myself. But perhaps we can get the Calypso singers to compose a song especially for us."

When he had pulled up near the employees quarters of the hotel, John cut the motor and turned, slipping an arm around Denise's shoulder.

"Time for me to ride off alone into the sunset," he quipped. "But I'll be back. Did you enjoy the day?"

"Tremendously! You plan marvelous surprises," Denise smiled.

He leaned forward, but his lips had no more than brushed hers when a chattering group of vacationers scrunched up the gravel path. Passing by, they eyed the young couple with amusement.

John drew back, trying not to look disgruntled. "Have to wait for a more opportune moment, I guess."

He walked around and assisted Denise out of the jeep. They strolled arm in arm to the door of the building.

"I'll call you soon," he promised. "Don't forget, we have a date for the fiesta."

Denise all but waltzed inside after he had gone. It had been a lovely, lovely day! Every single minute of it — except, she remembered, with a twinge of uneasiness, for the confrontation with Orestes in the cafe. But John had handled even that touchy encounter with diplomatic finesse.

She could hardly wait for the fiesta, when she would be seeing him again!

With the Mardi Gras lull a thing of the past, the Caribe Azure's popularity reached an all-time high. New bookings flooded the office, and many guests who had come for a week extended their stay to two or even three times that duration. Much of the extra work fell on the shoulders of Leon Perdigo, but the overflow of tourists affected the rest of the staff as well, from the maids and groundskeepers right down to the athletic instructors.

In recognition of this fact, Martin Lorrimer hired extra help. Denise, Natalie and Roger now each had several assistants, yet the girls found it more and more of a chore to spare the extra hours to work with Cartuga's school children. Even so, they doggedly continued with the program.

It seemed to Denise that even the tireless housekeeper, Mama Elena, was showing the strain of overwork. Her concern reached a peak when she bumped into Catalina Ruiz in the hall toward the middle of the week. The little Cartugan maid seemed to be reeling from fatigue!

"Here, let me help you," Denise cried in alarm. She flung open the door to Catalina's room, and half-carried her friend across to the bed. When she placed her hand on the girl's forehead, she had to choke back a gasp of dismay. Catalina was burning with fever!

She tugged blankets and spread them over the limp figure, then darted down to the telephone in the lounge. After placing a request for the hotel doctor to come as quickly as possible, she hurried back to sit beside Catalina.

Half an hour later Dr. Baca was able to offer some reassurance.

"She has contracted a rather nasty virus, but I've given her something to bring down the fever," he told Denise. "She should be back to normal after three or four days in bed. However,

I can't let her return to work for at least a week. I'll notify Senor Perdigo, so that he can assign a substitute in her place."

He left a bottle of capsules on the nightstand, with instructions that the patient swallow one every four hours. Since there was no nurse available, Denise and several other of the sick girl's friends took over her care.

Catalina remained feverish and half-incoherent for the next day and a half. However, when Denise tiptoed into the room on Friday morning, she found her friend sitting up in bed with a breakfast tray on her lap.

"Goodness, what a scare you gave us!" she exclaimed in relief. "I'm glad to see that you aren't looking quite so pale any more."

"It was kind of you to worry about me," Catalina said shyly. "I feel much stronger now. If you will take this tray, I can get up and dress."

"You'll do no such thing! Dr. Baca said you were to stay in bed for four days."

"Oh, but I cannot!" Catalina's voice was shrill with agitation. "I must be well for tonight!"

Denise tried to soothe her. "You'll be sicker than ever if you don't obey the doctor's orders. Here, finish your orange juice, then go back to sleep like a good patient."

Catalina swallowed the cool drink as she was told. But she looked highly distraught at the idea of remaining in bed much longer.

"Luis will be waiting for me tonight," she insisted. "Ask him; he will tell you. We must be there by nine o'clock!"

Denise had no time to stay and argue, since she was already overdue at the pool. "Just promise me you will rest until dinnertime," she pleaded. "We can worry about Luis and everything later."

Catalina gave her word. Walking rapidly across the pavilion, Denise wondered why her friend was so determined to climb out of a sick bed. Surely, a date with Luis couldn't be *that* important!

But once on duty, she had no opportunity to concentrate on anything except her job. Nowadays, even the Olympic-sized pool was usually overcrowded. This made it doubly hard for the lifeguards to anticipate possible dangers before they arose.

Toward the end of the morning, an elderly man slipped while climbing out of the water. His arms made frantic, windmill motions in the air. Before any of the nearby swimmers could grab him he fell, striking his head against the tile surfacing of the pool. Denise was at his side within seconds, staunching the flow of blood with a hastily-snatched towel. The cut was small but deep, and she personally assisted him to the doctor's office for medical attention.

Because of this accident, she missed her lunch hour entirely. Nor was there any chance of looking in on Catalina, as she had intended. She could only cross her fingers and hope that her friend was not doing anything foolhardy.

By the time she had finished the school children's last lesson of the day Denise was feeling both tired and hungry. She could think of nothing more inviting than an early dinner, a hot bath, and bed.

As it happened, the evening turned out quite differently.

Upon returning to the hotel, she peeked in at Catalina before heading for her own room. The girl appeared to be sleeping peacefully. Denise continued on down the hall, confident that the situation was under control. She showered and changed and, after searching in vain for Natalie, walked on to the dining room alone.

She had nearly finished her salad by the time the blonde girl hurried up to the table.

"Sorry to be late," Natalie said.

She reached for the menu, but the large card did not quite conceal the little smile that kept edging up on her lips. When she ordered, it was with an airy lack of attention to the food.

"Are you coming down with some ghastly disease, or simply looking smug?" Denise demanded at last.

"Neither, I hope," Natalie retorted virtuously. "How's your fish?"

"Filling, thank heaven. The way I feel right now, I could eat octopus. Raw."

Denise gave her attention to her plate, but she could scarcely help noticing that Natalie continued to look blandly secretive. It occurred to her that Vince Borden might have had something to do with Natalie's suddenly radiant appearance.

Natalie disappeared again soon after dinner. Denise lingered behind, chatting first with Roger Gates, then with Alphonso and Jose. She kept glancing toward the door, hoping to catch sight of Luis Figueroa so that she could tell him of Catalina's illness. But when another half hour had elapsed with no sign of the young chauffeur, she gave up the vigil and returned to the lounge. There she picked up an armload of magazines. An hour's reading would put her in the mood for sleep. Perhaps, she thought, Catalina, too, might enjoy perusing some light fiction.

Nothing could have been further from the truth.

The door to the maid's room was slightly ajar. Denise tapped lightly, then stuck her head around the corner. What she saw nearly caused her to drop the magazines.

"For goodness sakes! What are you doing up — and dressed?" she scolded.

Catalina paused in the act of arranging a scarf over her long black hair. "I kept my promise," she said. "Now I must go."

"But go where?" Denise was beginning to feel exasperated. "Look," she offered, "suppose I find Luis and tell him you've been sick. He'll be glad to postpone your date until another night."

Catalina jumped up, swaying unsteadily. She caught hold of the dressing table for support. "No, no! You do not understand. It is to Amalie we must go. Together. Otherwise — It is about our debt," she finished lamely.

Denise had no idea of whom or what Amalie was, but she knew desperation when she saw it. Catalina was already more than half hysterical. Briefly, she considered calling the doctor and keeping the girl there forcibly. But something told her this would only make matters worse.

"All right," she conceded. "If you're so dead set on leaving, I'll go with you. That way at least I can make sure you don't faint into the shrubbery!"

For some reason, this suggestion caused Catalina to look more frightened than ever. She shook her head emphatically, declaring that Denise's plan was unthinkable. But the fever had left her very weak, and after a few minutes she gave in with a sigh of resignation.

"Yes, then, if you promise not to interfere. You will do this?" she asked anxiously.

Denise nodded, by now completely baffled. Interfere with what?

Snatching the scarf from her own head, Catalina wound it around Denise's black hair, drawing it well forward so that her face was partially obscured. Then both girls pulled on dark, lightweight coats. A short time later they were hurrying down the path leading to the hotel's kitchen entrance.

Luis had been striding impatiently up and down. He started forward at their approach, then paused in alarm when he recognized

Denise. Catalina answered his abrupt question with a spurt of Spanish too rapid for the American girl to follow. Apparently she had explained about her illness, for Luis's expression changed to one of concern, and he helped her into the dilapidated old truck with tender care.

"Please — I will take care of her now," he said, turning back to Denise. "You need not worry."

"But I am worried," she insisted. "Can't you persuade Catalina to stay home in bed? She's been terribly sick."

Luis shook his head. "That is impossible. We —"

"I know," Denise groaned. "You must go. Okay, the nurse is coming too."

His dark eyes regarded her gravely. "Do as we say, then, and no harm will befall you."

With this enigmatic warning, he hopped into the driver's seat. Denise squeezed in beside Catalina, already beginning to regret her stubbornness. Where on earth were they going?

For more than half an hour the old truck bumped along a road which coiled and snaked through the foothills. With growing uneasiness Denise watched the last traces of the sunset vanish. Before they reached their destination the sky had darkened to the color of jet, unrelieved by stars or moon. Even the trees illuminated by the faint beams of the headlights seemed to reach menacingly out toward the truck.

Just as she felt she could not bear the suspense for an instant longer, Luis turned left onto a rutted trail which only an optimist could have described as a road. At that moment a weird sound reached Denise's ears, and her nervousness crystallized into solid fear. Her fingers turned ice cold from a terror which was no longer nameless.

Why, she berated herself, hadn't she guessed? It was so hideously obvious!

She swallowed hard, wishing she could drown out the throb of the *rada* drums which grew louder with every heartbeat. But there was no escaping the savage rhythm; it swelled to a raging pulse as Luis braked at the edge of the clearing.

Denise's knees wobbled as she forced herself to climb out of the truck. Fortunately, the voodoo ceremony had already begun. The gaze of every person present was directed unblinkingly toward the dancers who swayed and shuffled in and out of the *tonnelle,* a crude, thatched roof supported by slender poles. No one took any note of the newcomers who sank quietly down on a bench behind the last row of spectators.

The tempo of the drumbeat waned and the white-clad dancers, whom Catalina described as *hounsi,* or novices, took up a slow, repetitious chant. The very monotony of the simple phrases, repeated over and over again, lulled Denise's fears. She remembered that voodoo was, after all, merely a primitive form of worship. Even John had said that, except in rare instances, the ceremonies were harmless.

At first Luis and Catalina had kept glancing at her apprehensively. Soon, though, they gave their whole attention to the spectacle. Flickering torches provided the only light; still, Denise was careful to keep the scarf down to conceal much of her face. But as the minutes passed with no outcry being made against her presence, she was able to relax and view the proceedings with interest.

Painted gourds and streamers of red, blue, yellow and orange paper hung from the beams of the thatched *tonnelle,* and the center post supporting the roof was decorated in colors of red, rose and green. She learned later that this sacred post was the home of Papa Legba, the spirit who was invoked first to "open the gate" for the emergence of the other spirits, or *loas.* To the rear of the *tonnelle* was a sort of altar, or *pe,* covered with exotically decorated jars of various shapes and sizes. It was in these jars, Catalina told her in a reverent whisper, that the *loas* resided until summoned forth.

Almost imperceptibly, now, the tempo of the drums increased. The feet of the *hounsi* kept pace; in turn each of the dancers kissed the ground, then sprinkled a few drops of water around the center post.

Denise became aware of a strange new scent permeating the air. Somewhere close by incense was being burned. As the heady odor wafted over the throng, one of the *hounsi,* a native girl no older than herself, suddenly stiffened. Denise watched in horror as the girl's head began shaking violently from side to side. A fit of trembling seized her entire body; her eyes rolled wildly and she whirled into a frenzied dance. Again and again she shouted out the same name. "Legba! Legba!"

"The spirit has possessed her!" Luis cried in awe.

Denise found that her own hands were trembling. Not for an instant did she believe that the girl was really possessed, but the writhing contortions were frightening to watch. In an effort to remain calm, she twined her fingers together until they ached.

Superstition and the power of suggestion went hand-in-hand, she reasoned to herself. The eerie setting, the throb of drums and the incense had no doubt all combined to excite the peoples' imagination, leaving them receptive to the idea that a supernatural being had entered their midst.

In spite of this common-sense appraisal, the atmosphere of tense expectancy was contagious. She felt a sharp stab of relief when at last the dancer dropped from sheer exhaustion.

But this sensation was short-lived. Rather than relaxing after the state of near frenzy which the whirling exhibition had seemed to inspire in them, the spectators now appeared more excited than ever.

"Amalie! Amalie!" they chanted in one voice,

as the drumbeat swelled and roared to a thunderous fanfare.

Suddenly, as mysteriously as if she were herself a spirit, a woman appeared to float forward from the depths of the *tonnelle*. Although she was taller than most men, and of ponderous girth, Denise had the impression that the woman's bare feet scarcely touched the ground.

So this was the *mambo*. The voodoo high priestess!

The woman who approached carried a tall, slender candle. Its tongue of flame sputtered mere inches from her face, casting flickering shadows across her white costume and the long ropes of colored beads which swayed rhythmically as she walked. More beads were wound around a painted gourd in her other hand.

All this Denise took in at a glance, before her full attention riveted on the *mambo*'s bright, jet-black eyes. That unwavering gaze seemed to penetrate to the very rim of the crowd. For one panic-stricken moment she felt those all-seeing eyes touch hers — touch and cling with a commanding power — before traveling on.

Denise's earlier terror came flooding back. She could never have explained the sudden chill of fear which enveloped her; it was instinctive, but dreadfully real. Some inner caution warned that the woman who stood haughtily regarding the crowd was evil — and utterly ruthless!

She shrank down in her seat, barely noticing the next part of the program. Another dance had begun, involving a quartet of flagbearers and an agile youth who whirled around them brandishing a huge machete, but Denise had lost interest in the ceremony. She could only pray that it would end soon!

Presently, the *mambo* had the stage to herself again. The eyes of everyone present riveted upon her as she took up a bowl of corn meal. Sprinkling it, a pinch at a time, in quick, deft motions, she drew a large, intricate design on the dirt floor.

Catalina murmured that this *veve* was the symbol of one of the *loas*. "The spirits will be pleased," she murmured. "Soon they will all walk amongst us."

Denise stole a look at her friend. The expression on Catalina's thin face was one of solemn dedication. For the first time Denise realized what John had meant when he spoke of the difficulties of battling this superstitious belief. Amalie had these people completely mesmerized!

Apparently they were approaching the climax of the ritual, for the drums, which had temporarily fallen silent, now resumed their throbbing beat. Denise shivered as vibrations from the earth-shaking sounds filled the air. When a pair of chickens were brought forward to be sacrificed, she spun aside in disgust, unable to watch the horrible spectacle any longer!

A crescent moon had risen, shedding a pale light down to mingle with the harsh illumination of the torches. As she turned, Denise was astonished to glimpse movement among the ring of trees encircling the clearing. She wondered which of the spectators had been brave enough to leave before the ceremony was ended. A second later, she saw another dark shadow drift forward to join the first.

It was their air of stealth which most piqued Denise's curiosity. No more than five yards separated the two men from the back row of benches, yet the drums effectively drowned their conversation. The heavy foliage of the trees blotted out everything except their shadows, making identification impossible.

As she continued to peer backwards, it dawned on Denise that the conspirators were having an argument. One of them was much taller than the other, yet it seemed to be the smaller man who was giving the orders.

At that instant the drum roll abruptly ceased. In the sudden silence, a few of the angry, whispered words reached her ears.

"You fool!" the shorter of the two hissed in Spanish. "Can't you realize how dangerous —"

An indistinguishable rumble of protest came from his companion.

Denise found herself straining to hear more. There had been a disturbing familiarity about that first voice. She was convinced that in other circumstances she would have recognized it easily. But listen as she would, she managed to catch only another disjointed phrase or two.

"... ruin everything! ... have to wait until ... not long ..."

The last words faded out as the men moved farther back into the forest. Denise cautiously edged back to her original position, but her mind was racing furiously.

That tantalizingly familiar voice belonged to someone she knew. She was positive! But who among her acquaintances, would have come here? Luis and Catalina were still beside her —

Denise came to with a start, suddenly aware that the crowd was beginning to disperse. Yet her friends remained stubbornly in their seats. Only when the last of the footsteps had shuffled past did Catalina rise. Then, instead of turning toward the truck, she walked forward, toward the *mambo*.

Had Luis not clamped a hand across her wrist in warning, Denise would have cried out in protest.

There was something frighteningly trance-like about Catalina's expression. This look was reflected on the faces of the others who approached the *mambo,* twelve or fifteen of them. Denise was bewildered to note that they all walked with the same, slow-motion gait. It was as if they were in a state of hypnosis!

Each person in turn bowed ceremoniously to Amalie, then stooped and placed something in a wicker basket at the base of the *tonnelle*'s center pole. A puff of wind tilted the basket, furnishing Denise with a glimpse of crisp, new bills inside.

She frowned angrily. That unexpected view explained a great many things — Catalina's nervousness about missing the ceremony, the postponement of her marriage to Luis — Their money was pledged to Amalie!

Yet most people had left without making a donation. Why was Catalina among the chosen few?

Denise restrained her questions, realizing that this was hardly the time to start delving into the mystery. She caught her breath as Catalina started back up the slope toward them. Sheer determination had carried the girl this far, but the strain of the evening on top of her recent illness was obviously taking its toll.

Beads of perspiration had broken out on Catalina's forehead. In the half-light, her eyes looked unnaturally large. Each swaying step seemed to be achieved only after a tremendous effort.

Luis darted out onto the footpath, and caught the fainting girl in his arms.

"Follow me," he ordered, tossing the words over his shoulder to Denise.

In her haste to do so, the scarf slipped away from her hair and dropped to the ground. She wasted precious seconds fumbling for it. Straightening up, she thrust the square of material haphazardly over her head and plunged into the underbrush.

Luis had already hurried several yards along the rough, uneven trail. Denise raced after him, terrified of being left alone in this eerie place. So intent was she on joining her friends that not until she had stumbled to within a few feet of him did she notice the young giant of a man who stood, arms akimbo, at the edge of the path.

Orestes was staring directly at her!

Chapter Nine

The man who regarded all Americans as his archenemies stood between her and escape!

Denise faltered for only a second. Sensing that hesitation could prove fatal, she choked down the panic which threatened to paralyze her, and sped past him with her head bent low. She felt his curious gaze on her back as she pelted down the footpath, but no power on earth could have made her turn for a second glimpse of him. Maybe the scarf had concealed enough of her face to prevent recognition!

"Let's get out of here!" she gasped, tumbling into the truck beside the semi-conscious Catalina.

Luis, too, seemed eager to depart. To Denise's relief, the old engine hiccuped into action as soon as he pressed the starter. It was some minutes, though, before she managed to stop trembling and was able to think coherently again.

The trail had been dark, she reassured herself. But not dark enough to prevent her from identifying Orestes. A shudder iced its way up her spine as she remembered the glint of his piercing black eyes. Eyes like Amalie's!

The two were obviously mother and son!

With a gulp, Denise recalled John Westcott's

description of the *mambo* who had fled Haiti, only to resume the practice of her black magic on the people of Cartuga. Her own first glimpse of Amalie had convinced her that the woman was evil. She felt positive that John was right when he declared that the *mambo* used blackmail and terror to control her superstitious followers!

That sight of Orestes lurking by the path had also evoked another memory — that of two men meeting stealthily in the trees behind the clearing. One of them had all but dwarfed the other. The very hugeness of the shadow he had cast convinced her that it was Orestes whom she had seen. Orestes and one other. Someone she knew. Someone who had argued about danger; who had insisted that a plan be delayed —

If only she had heard enough to know what they were talking about!

On the seat beside her, Catalina moaned weakly. Denise propped the girl's sagging body into a more comfortable position, then shot an accusing glance at Luis.

"The fever has returned. You must have known what a terrible strain this evening would place on her! Why didn't you stop her from coming?"

"Amalie would have been angered," he shivered. "There are spells —"

"Spells don't work unless you believe in them!" Denise protested. "Luis, that horrid woman can't really hurt you. It's positively sinful to keep on giving her money!"

He hunched his shoulders, a gesture which hinted of stubborn fear.

"Be quiet! Amalie can do anything she likes," he insisted. "Did she not give Catalina a charm that guaranteed we would be hired to work at the hotel? Many others have no jobs. Now we repay Amalie by donating half our salaries to the *loas* for one year."

"That's highway robbery!"

And blackmail, Denise added to herself. A lot of good money would do the spirits! But she knew that she could never convince Luis that he and Catalina had been hired on their merits alone.

The chilling terror evoked by the voodoo ritual had already begun to fade from her mind. Now that Denise could look back on the night's events without shaking, she found a great many questions to ask. One was especially troublesome.

"Catalina seemed normal enough until the ceremoney was over. Then she — she seemed to go into a trance. So did the few others who remained. What happened?"

Luis refused to meet her eyes. "Amalie's *Wanga* is all-powerful," he mumbled. "At the snap of her fingers, we could be turned into zombies. No one dares question the *mambo!*"

Denise had heard of zombies, "the walking dead." She remembered that the state of these unfortunates resembled a condition of deep hypnosis. Her eyes widened.

Hypnosis! Of course, that was how Amalie managed it!

"I'll bet she hypnotized Catalina when she gave her that charm," Denise reasoned.

Then, all the *mambo* needed to do was snap her fingers. Catalina and the others would respond automatically to the post-hypnotic suggestion. Amalie could put them back into a trance — or order them to do anything she chose. Like sleep-walkers, they would obey her instructions, without even realizing what was happening!

Denise sighed, and wondered what on earth to do. Perhaps Martin Lorrimer could persuade the authorities to take action against Amalie. Somehow, though, she doubted it. The police would need proof. And who would dare to testify against the *mambo?* Everyone was completely terrified of her "powers!"

"John was right," she told herself. "We'll have to prove Amalie is a fraud, before these people will stop believing in her."

Easier said than done!

Denise had pool duty over the weekend. In addition, she spent many of her leisure hours helping care for Catalina. His patient's relapse baffled Dr. Baca; this time he absolutely forbade any activity for several days, and warned of dire consequences to her health should she attempt to get out of bed before he gave permission.

Catalina was too ill to offer any objection.

Mama Elena and the other girls in the building again cooperated in carrying trays and smoothing sheets. But it was Denise, with more free time than most, who spent long hours in the sick girl's room, reading or just thinking while Catalina tossed feverishly in the bed.

After much inner debate, Denise had decided to keep the events of that Friday evening to herself. Senor Lorrimer was a modern man with no patience for superstition. She feared that should he learn of his employees' connection with the *mambo*, he might dismiss them from his employ.

That would only make matters worse!

Denise wished fervently that she could talk the matter over with John. But he was spending a few days in the mountains, assisting the owner of a coffee plantation with an engineering matter. She had no choice except to wait until the coming weekend before seeking his advice.

Another point which troubled her was the identity of Orestes' companion that night at the ritual. Try as she would, she was unable to link a name or face with the hauntingly familiar voice she had overheard. Could the conspirators have been planning a crime? She had an uneasy glimmering of suspicion that their plan had some relation to the Caribe Azure.

Because that voice had belonged to someone here at the hotel!

Denise sighed. Trying to outguess the plotters was futile. Those few, angry words had proved nothing. And yet —

What a shame the *rada* drums hadn't ceased a moment sooner!

As Martin Lorrimer had promised, the Independence Day fiesta was the most memorable celebration ever held on the island of Cartuga.

In more ways than one.

By mid-afternoon, everyone associated with the Caribe Azure had entered into the holiday spirit. Hotel guests and staff members alike joined in the revelry. Rhythmic Latin music filled every corner of the pavilion, and already the Calypso singers were mingling with the throng, delighting their listeners with hilarious verses composed on the spur of the moment.

In spite of the happy conviviality that sparkled all around her, Denise was feeling rather left out of things. Natalie and Vince appeared to be sharing a secret, Mama Elena and the head chef were in the process of winning a dance competition, and even Roger seemed unusually carefree and talkative as he escorted one of Leon Perdigo's pretty daughters to the buffet table.

Her sense of exclusion vanished abruptly, though, when she caught sight of John Westcott making his way with determination through the crowd.

"It's been much too long since I've seen you," he said, taking both her hands in his. "Let's dance, shall we? I don't want to waste a minute of our day."

Denise gave him a radiant smile. Now that they were together again, she wanted nothing more than to forget the anxieties of the past week and simply concentrate on enjoying his company.

For an hour or so she managed to do just that. In between dances, she introduced John to a number of her friends and acquaintances. Myra Hendricks beamed her approval on the young couple, and invited them to join her for a glass of punch. They accepted, and lingered to chat a brief time. Then, as she turned to set her glass back on the table, Denise spied Catalina and Luis sitting together in a quiet corner of the pavilion. The memory of the frightening experience she had shared with them came rushing back to trouble her.

"I need your advice about something," she said, when they had excused themselves. "I don't suppose it's really urgent, but —"

John's smiling grey eyes sobered as they surveyed her earnest face. "You'll never convince me in that tone of voice," he warned.

He led her away from the milling throng, beneath the archway and up onto the for-once deserted sundeck rimming the pool.

"All right, out with it," he ordered, slowing his pace to a companionable stroll. He slipped an arm around her waist. "You sounded entirely too serious for someone who is supposed to be enjoying a fiesta. What's the matter?"

Denise took a deep breath, aware that anyone

who hadn't lived in these islands would probably break into peals of laughter.

"It's this darned voodoo!" she blurted. "Sort of accidentally, I attended one of their ceremonies last week."

Not a hint of laughter crossed John's dumbfounded face. He halted, gaping at her in astonishment. "Accidentally?"

"Maybe we had better sit down," Denise suggested. "It's rather complicated."

John dropped into the deck chair next to hers. He listened in silent thoughtfulness while she described Catalina's illness, and her own insistence on accompanying the girl. Not until she mentioned the *mambo*'s name did he break in with an exclamation.

"Amalie! But she's the woman I was telling you about. That young thug we met in the cafe is her son!"

Goosebumps prickled Denise's skin. "I encountered him again, out there. And that isn't all...."

"You haven't any notion what Orestes and this other man were discussing?" John frowned, when she had finished recounting the tale.

"No. I only heard that much because the drumming stopped so suddenly. Even that little bit was enough to make me suspicious," Denise said. "Do you think we ought to warn Senor Lorrimer?"

"Of what?" John shook his head. "There's nothing concrete. We don't even know for sure that a crime is being planned. And the only hook-up with the Caribe Azure is a voice that you think sounded familiar!

"About this hold Amalie has on your friend — that's something else again," he continued pensively. "It sounds like a spooky sort of blackmail to me. If we could get even one of those people she's hypnotized to sign a complaint, the police could prosecute her on that charge alone."

Denise dredged up a rueful smile. If Luis and Catalina were typical examples of the *mambo*'s followers, she admitted, it seemed highly unlikely that anyone bold enough to complain would be found.

"Well, I'll look into it, anyway," John promised. He got to his feet, and held out a hand to Denise. But instead of releasing her, he drew her closer.

"You're getting awfully involved with these people," he murmured. "First the kids' swim lessons, and now this problem of Catalina's. If you don't stop, you're going to find it tough to turn your back on this country when the time comes to leave."

"I'm not sure I'll ever want to do that."

The admission surprised even Denise. Not more than a month or two ago, she had tried to put all thoughts of John Westcott out of her mind because of uncertainty that his way of life could ever be hers.

Yet now the words had come from her heart. She *was* involved with Cartuga. Its tropical charm had infiltrated her defenses, just as surely as John's personality had melted her reservations about his career.

She had fallen in love with both him and the island!

This time when he kissed her, there was no one to interrupt. A moment or two later he stepped back, but he kept her hand tucked firmly in his. As they walked through the gathering twilight together, Denise knew that the kiss had held a promise for the future.

The volume of noise in the pavilion seemed to have increased a hundredfold during their absence. A few skyrockets had already been shot off to brighten the gathering dusk, and everyone was eagerly anticipating the major display. Meanwhile, voices rose more shrilly, and the band played more raucously than ever before.

John and Denise made their way to the long, lavishly decorated buffet table and helped themselves from the tempting array of delicacies. They had no more than found a place to sit when Martin Lorrimer, glowing with pride as he surveyed the throng, ascended the bandstand.

"I had prepared a lengthy, patriotic speech," the hotel owner joked, when the crowd had quieted enough to allow his words to be heard. "However, I believe I will allow the music and fireworks to speak for Independence Day. And in place of rhetoric, I have the honor of announcing the impending marriage of two persons who have helped make this fiesta — and this hotel — such a resounding success. Miss Natalie Engstromm and Mr. Vincent Borden!"

When Natalie, looking petite and radiant in a sunshine yellow gown, made a brief appearance on stage with her new fiance, Denise applauded until her hands tingled. Apparently, she thought, the surprise had been planned for some time. The next eruption of fireworks outlined a many-tiered wedding cake against the now completely darkened sky.

"So that was the great surprise!" she exclaimed to John. "No wonder they've both been acting zany the past few days. What a dumbbell I was not to guess!"

Denise's first impulse had been to rush over and congratulate her friends, but this intention was forestalled by preparations for the limbo dancing. All tables were pushed back from the center of the pavilion, clearing a large circle for the event. Everyone immediately left their chairs and clustered around. The mass of spectators made it all but impossible for anyone to cross from one side of the entertainment area to the other.

"Here's something you won't want to miss," John insisted, urging her forward. "Talk about limber! You'd swear some of these dancers had traded backbones with a boa constrictor, the way they slither under that bar!"

Contenting herself with a wave to Natalie, Denise took advantage of a gap near the stage to get a front-row view of the performance. John squeezed in close behind her, pointing out the two vertical poles which had been set up, and the horizontal bar that would be gradually lowered as the dancers strove to outdo each other in feats of agility.

The professional entertainers made the first few passes beneath the bar look ridiculously easy. But as the wooden barrier dropped lower and lower, even they began to show the strain which their muscles were enduring.

Caught up in the excitement of each new triumph, Denise gasped as the bar slipped into its last notch, mere inches from the floor.

"Not even a cat could wriggle under that!" she declared.

John chuckled. "Wait and see!"

A native girl stepped confidently forward. She danced a complete circle around the vertical poles, her flying bare feet keeping perfect time to the staccato throb of the Calypso drums. Then, little by little, her pencil-slim body bent backwards. Her spine arched sinuously, until her long black hair dragged along the ground. Not once did her bobbing shoulders miss a beat of the music.

Denise exhaled, wondering how long she had been holding her breath. It seemed impossible that any human being could control her body so rigidly, yet make it appear that every movement was pure, fluid grace!

Still the dancer sank lower. Not until her legs

were completely doubled did she begin a steady but tantalizingly slow advance beneath the bar. By this time the entire audience was cheering and applauding wildly. When the girl's forehead at last emerged, without having so much as grazed the bar, Denise found that she was hoarse from having shouted encouragement.

"What a performance!" Her blue eyes laughed vivaciously up at John. "That girl could make a fortune on television!"

Anything after that spectacular feat was bound to be an anticlimax. Nevertheless, a number of the hotel guests clamored to try the limbo dance for themselves. Wedged in as they were by a solid mass of humanity, John and Denise had no alternative except to stay and watch the amateur attempts.

A few of the younger women did creditably well the first few times under, although they lacked the contortionist abilities of the professionals. Gradually, the spectators lost interest and started to drift away. Denise, who was still anxious to speak with Natalie, was looking for a passage through the crowd when a plump, middle-aged lady who was spending the entire winter at the Caribe Azure decided to try her luck at the limbo dance.

She muffled a giggle, recalling that Mrs. Duff was usually so tightly corseted that she had difficulty bending forwards, let alone back!

"Oh my, I hope she doesn't hurt herself," she murmured apprehensively.

The words had scarcely left her lips when the would-be dancer lost her balance and thudded to the ground. Mrs. Duff squeaked in surprise and embarrassment, but her well-cushioned frame was hardly bruised. Denise and John, along with several of those still remaining to watch, hurried over to help her up.

"Goodness! I guess that will teach me to remember my age," Mrs. Duff laughed at herself.

She made dusting-off motions at the skirt of her long chiffon dress. Then, as she glanced down, her arm froze in mid-air, and she stared increduously at her wrist.

"My diamond bracelet!" she wailed. "It — it's shattered!"

Chapter Ten

Denise focused disbelievingly on the glittering bauble. She had had an opportunity to admire the bracelet on several previous occasions, since Mrs. Duff habitually wore it for evening affairs. Twenty enormous square-cut diamonds were surrounded by scallops of smaller stones, each a perfect, many-faceted jewel in its own right. The bracelet had obviously cost many thousands of dollars.

She simply could not believe the sight which now met her eyes. More than half of the gems were cracked and splintered, and two of the stones, which had apparently smacked directly on the concrete floor when the woman lost her balance, had disintegrated into powdery white dust!

"Oh, but that's impossible," Denise gasped faintly. "Diamonds don't —"

"These did. Hush."

John Westcott mouthed the warning in her ear, then stepped forward to take charge. There were murmurs of surprise and curiosity among the bystanders, but Mrs. Duff was still too stunned to protest when he guided her away from the pavilion and into the hotel lobby.

Trailing in their wake, Denise caught sight of

Martin Lorrimer standing on the fringes of the crowd. In response to her frantic gesture, he hurried inside to join the group.

"Is something —" he began, but before he could complete the question, Mrs. Duff thrust her trembling arm in front of his face.

"My diamonds! Look what's happened to my diamonds!"

One glance was all Senor Lorrimer needed to send a hasty summons for Ramon Helas, the jeweler who managed the flourishing little boutique shop in the hotel's arcade, where both costume pieces and gems of great value could be purchased.

By the time the jeweler had been located, Mrs. Duff had launched into a full-scale bout of hysterics. Denise, trying to quiet her, peered across the desk while Senor Helas conducted a brief examination of the ruined bracelet.

"But — but these are not diamonds," he stuttered, removing the magnifying lens from his eye. "The stones are glass, nothing more. I do not understand —"

"Glass!" Mrs. Duff wailed indignantly. "How dare you! That bracelet was appraised and insured for twelve thousand dollars! I want to know what's happened to my diamonds!"

After this outburst, it took the combined efforts of everyone present to soothe the distraught woman. But Denise's thoughts were far away from the comforting phrases she murmured; absent-mindedly she moved aside when

Dr. Baca arrived to administer a sedative to Mrs. Duff.

Something like this had happened before! Frowning intently at the wall, she felt absolutely convinced that this was so. Another time, another place — but when?

Suddenly, the elusive memory solidified. Denise caught her breath. Yes, that was it! She waited until Mrs. Duff had been led away, then tugged urgently at John's coat-sleeve.

"Listen! I think I have a clue to this puzzle!"

She could not have attracted the men's attention more quickly had she tossed a grenade into their midst.

"You mean you *know* how diamonds are turned into glass?" Senor Lorrimer queried, with a hint of sarcasm.

"No, not that." Denise shook her head impatiently. "But I'm positive that this very same thing has occurred at least once before. I heard about it at the New Orleans airport, the day I arrived in Cartuga."

In the bedlam of the reservations line, voices had shrilled out over one another. She strained to recall the exact words which had been used. It was all so long ago....

"Some people were talking about a diamond necklace that had been stolen," she told them. "The strangest part was that the owner didn't realize there'd been a theft until she dropped the necklace. Then it turned out that her 'diamonds' were glass!"

Ramon Helas snapped his fingers. "Yes, yes, it is true," he agreed. "I myself read of this in the newspaper. Cheap imitations were substituted for the real gems, but the copy was so faultlessly made that only an expert could tell the difference. What is more," he added significantly, "the thief was never apprehended!"

"Holy Mother!" Martin Lorrimer groaned. "Could it be —"

In the portentous silence which followed, an even more appalling notion occurred to Denise.

"Myra Hendricks' necklace," she gulped. "Oh, my word! I wonder if that could be the explanation. . . ."

"Honey, if you're just trying to scare us, we've had enough thrills for tonight," John sighed. "What's all this about a necklace?"

"I saw it," she insisted. "Roger Gates did, too — in a shop window in Port-Au-Prince during Mardi Gras. Roger laughed at me when I insisted it was hers. Of course, I felt silly when I returned to the hotel and found Mrs. Hendricks wearing the necklace herself. That's why I never mentioned it. But the two pieces were absolutely identical!"

She glanced up at Leon Perdigo, who had entered the office while the discussion was taking place. "Besides, there was that peculiar incident last February when the necklace vanished out of her suite, then turned up a short time later!"

The hotel manager wrung his pudgy hands. "I

remember," he groaned. "We placed the blame on a faulty bureau drawer."

"I believe that is what we were meant to think," Denise said. "The thief could have entered the room while Mrs. Hendricks was down at the pool. That was the day she nearly drowned. He wouldn't have been expecting her to return so quickly. When I brought her upstairs, the necklace was missing — but half an hour later it had been returned!"

"Time enough to photograph it in detail," John remarked glumly.

Ramon Helas agreed that this was a logical assumption. In that way the forgers could reproduce the gems exactly. "When the cutting and polishing of the duplicate had been achieved, they would need only a minute to substitute one for the other. And since the weight and luster of the two pieces of jewelry were the same, who would ever suspect?"

"My poor hotel! How its reputation will suffer," Martin Lorrimer lamented.

For a moment, silence filled the room. Then, with a gesture of helplessness, the Caribe Azure's owner faced up to the situation. "By the grace of God, what we suspect will be proven untrue," he said hopefully. "But we must know for sure. Would you be so good, Miss O'Shea, to find Mrs. Hendricks and ask her to join us here?"

An hour afterward their worst fears had been confirmed. The shattered "diamond" bracelet and the costly emerald and ruby necklace were fabricated from the same deceptive — and worthless — material.

Solid glass!

"There isn't much chance that we can keep this from exploding into a scandal now," John said gloomily, as he and Denise strolled back toward the employees' wing through the velvety tropical night. "What a finale to the fiesta!"

"Heaven only knows how many other substitutions have been made — or whether the thief is even still in Cartuga or not." A chill brushed Denise's bare shoulders. "He must be a regular Houdini to regard locked doors so casually."

John squeezed her consolingly. "Try not to worry about it. The police are already checking on that shop in Haiti. With luck, that could prove a valuable lead. And by tomorrow this place will be overrun with insurance investigators. The hotel will weather the storm somehow."

"I hope you're right."

Denise said goodnight to John at the doorway, then trudged down the hall to her room. Her thoughts were far from optimistic. Unless the gems were speedily recovered, the Caribe Azure's good name might be blemished forever. And by this time the thief could have smuggled his booty halfway across the world!

That night, for the first time in a week, her restless sleep was disturbed by dreams. Denise awoke in a tangle of blankets with her heart still thudding wildly. Its throb recalled the beat of *rada* drums, and even though dazzling morning sunlight now flooded her bedroom, the nightmare had not completely faded with the darkness. Amalie had been present in her dream, she remembered. Orestes, too, and the man who had whispered with him about danger. . . .

Denise struggled upright, wondering why her subconscious hadn't concentrated on dreams of mysteriously vanishing jewels. Surely, the crisis facing the hotel was more urgent than anything to do with unknown plans or voodoo rituals, no matter how eerie.

She shrugged into robe and slippers and started toward the bathroom. Unless, she thought suddenly, there was some link between the two — some relationship too fantastic to be considered seriously outside the shadowed world of sleep.

She turned the shower on full-blast, jeering at the melodramatic tenor of this notion. Voodoo and jewel thefts? Perhaps, she decided with a giggle, one of the *loas* had crept inside locked doors and stolen the gems!

On her way to breakfast, Denise nearly collided with Natalie in the hall.

"Goodness, what are *you* doing out of bed before ten o'clock on a Sunday morning?" she laughed.

"There has to be a first time for everything," Natalie yawned. "To tell the truth, I was too worried to sleep. Poor Vince is terribly upset. I don't believe he got to bed at all last night. He says the most brilliant public relations man in the world couldn't gloss over anything as serious as these jewel thefts."

Denise nodded, aware of the problem which confronted Vince. No matter how many advantages a resort boasted, the public would hardly flock to a spot where robbers operated unchecked!

"Let's hope they solve the case soon," she agreed. "I wanted to tell you at the fiesta how delighted I was to hear the news, but the pavilion was so mobbed I couldn't get through. Have you set a date for the wedding yet?"

"We *had* talked about June. I don't know, now." Natalie plodded dejectedly along, hands thrust deep into the pockets of her sports skirt. "I suppose it's possible that the hotel might fold. Then we'd all lose our jobs, and we couldn't afford to be married for ages."

"Nonsense!" Denise packed a conviction into her tone that she was far from feeling. "Senor Lorrimer would never allow the Caribe Azure to close. And I'm sure he realizes that good publicity is more important now than ever before. Vince can always think up something to put the place back on the map."

But Natalie's pessimism had shadowed her own mood, and not even the sight of John Westcott emerging from the office later that morning could completely restore her cheerfulness.

"Hi! Is there any news?" she called, hurrying

to catch up with him.

"Plenty — all the wrong sort." His brown hair was rumpled, and his grey eyes looked heavy from lack of sleep. "They've discovered three new thefts so far this morning. And the policeman in charge has just received a bulletin from the Haitian authorities. They were too late to nab the owner of that shop. Apparently he padlocked the place the day after Mardi Gras — and nobody's seen him since!"

"Oh, good grief! Maybe he came along that morning and heard me making a fuss about the necklace," Denise moaned.

John shrugged. "Anything's possible, I guess. And unless the time element is a pretty fishy coincidence, the man's disappearance does substantiate your theory that it was the real necklace you saw over there."

Denise felt more positive than ever that this had been the case. She walked along with John as far as the parking lot, asking questions about the shop owner's identity and his past record. As yet, only sketchy information was available, he told her. The man's name was Esteban Madero, and several times in the past few years he had been arrested on charges of receiving stolen merchandise.

"But you and Roger Gates are the only two people who remember having seen the necklace in that window," he grimaced. "And even Roger can't give an accurate description of it. He says he wasn't feeling well that day, and was mainly concerned with getting to the airport on time." He kicked absent-mindedly at the gravel. "Whether the jewels were real or fake, they couldn't have been displayed for very long or the neighboring businessmen would have noticed."

"Possibly he only took a chance on putting it out in the open because of Mardi Gras," Denise surmised. "With all the tourists jamming Port-Au-Prince that week, he could have hoped to make a quick sale."

"Well, it's gone now. And so is Madero."

Denise leaned thoughtfully against the jeep while John fished in the glove compartment for a sheaf of documents he had obtained from the Customs officials. These records listed items of value which had been brought into Cartuga during the past six months. Using them as a guide, the investigators hoped to pinpoint every theft which had been committed.

"I don't believe this man Madero is the thief who's been operating at the hotel," she remarked pensively. "A stranger would be noticed immediately here. But his Haitian nationality makes me wonder whether he mightn't be connected with Amalie and Orestes Tigue. They came from Haiti. And unless I'm wrong about that voice being familiar, there's a link between Orestes and the Caribe Azure."

John grinned at her. "Still worrying about mysterious voices?"

"Well, it *could* have been the jewel thefts they were discussing that night!" Denise waved away a wasp. "John, what does Orestes do? For a living, I mean. Even though his mother is the *mambo,* he must have some trade or profession of his own."

"Honey, I wish you'd forget about this voodoo business. Really, it isn't safe."

John snapped a rubber band around the folder, and straightened up. "I'll check into Orestes' background when I get a spare minute," he promised. "But unless we learn that he's an apprentice second-story man, I think we'll be further ahead by concentrating on the hotel angle. The thief *had* to spend quite a long time here in order to make all those switches. That knowledge is bound to be a tremendous help when it comes to checking criminal records."

As Denise followed him back up the path, she caught sight of Luis industriously polishing one of the hotel limousines. She waved to him, wondering whether he had been close enough to overhear their conversation. Not that it mattered, she decided. By now everyone even remotely connected with the Caribe Azure must know about the thefts. They would be lucky if the news didn't explode into mainland headlines by noon!

"Are the police going on the assumption that the thief is still here?" she asked.

"They're hoping that he hasn't left the country yet," John nodded. "He seems to be a pretty audacious fellow. Could be he was counting on the duplicate jewels covering his movements until he'd had time to make a million-dollar haul!"

He glanced around, and lowered his voice. "They plan to search the entire premises right after lunch. Practically the whole Cartugan police force will take place in the hunt. If the loot hasn't been smuggled out, they'll find it!"

"I certainly wish them luck. And you, too!"

Denise sent an encouraging smile his way as they parted in the lobby. This might be the trickiest job of his career, she thought sympathetically — trying to placate five wealthy, irate women who had been victimized by a crook!

Idly, she wandered down by the pool, but the rippling expanse of cool, blue water was nearly deserted. Alfonso appeared to be having a lonesome morning. The tennis courts, too, were empty of players. About to start back, she saw Natalie emerging from the equipment cabana, and she waited by the gate until her friend caught up with her.

"What a dull day!" Natalie grumbled. "I've just spent the last hour looking for racquets that need to be re-strung. There isn't a thing to do!"

Denise observed that the hotel guests seemed to be finding gossip an absorbing occupation. Wherever they looked, little knots of people were clustered together, excitedly exchanging one rumor for another.

Rather than be drawn into any of the chattering groups, the girls detoured around the side of the main building. A friendly cry hailed them when they rounded the corner. Startled, they glanced up to see Roger Gates trudging in from the direction of the greens. A battered old golf bag was slung across his shoulders, and his face looked flushed from the exertion of carrying it.

"Have they moved the fairway?" Denise laughed.

An expression of disgust flickered across his features. "No, it's still out there — jammed with foursomes all swapping the latest juicy tidbits. I decided that I'd take the boat over to the Isle — practice my putting in peace and quiet."

"That's undoubtedly the only place you'll get any today," Natalie remarked. "There must be fifty policemen inside — all ready to start tearing the hotel apart in search of those jewels!"

Roger let the bag of clubs slump to the ground while he mopped his brow. "Why don't you girls come along with me?" he suggested. "We could get a picnic lunch from the kitchen and make a day of it."

The proposal sounded highly inviting to Denise. Even Natalie, whose fear of water amounted to an obsession, wavered indecisively.

"Vince is up to his ears in newspaper reporters," she admitted. "And I suppose there's nothing we can do to help here. . . ."

"We'd only be in the way." Roger glanced at his watch. "Make up your minds. Shall I go see what I can finagle out of the chef in the way of chicken sandwiches?"

"Oh, all right." Natalie gave in.

Denise, too, nodded her acceptance. "You two go ahead," she urged them. "It will only take me a minute to get my bathing suit."

Her footsteps scrunched loudly on the gravel as she hurried down the path. Like the pool and the tennis courts the vicinity of the employees' wing seemed unusually quiet. She guessed that most of the staff would be gathered in the recreation lounge, discussing the calamitous discoveries of the past few hours with as much avidity as the guests had displayed.

After all this tumult, she decided, the serenity of the Isle would be a distinct relief!

Her hand was actually on the doorknob of her room before she realized that she was, after all, not quite alone in the building.

From someplace nearby had come a gasp of pure terror!

Denise froze. The sound was not repeated. The whole wing seemed wrapped in an oppressive silence.

But there had been a noise —

For endless seconds she stood riveted to the carpet, not moving, scarcely daring to breathe. It *could* have been her imagination. But after all that had been happening lately —

Suddenly, her doubts were resolved. A soft moan reached her ears, a moan which was almost simultaneous with the thud of a heavy burden striking the floor.

Denise whirled. A rapid half-dozen steps brought her to the door of Catalina's room. She flung it open — then had to swallow hard to choke down the cry of horror which rose in her throat.

Catalina lay motionless on the floor. But it was not this so much, as the object she held clenched in her outflung hand, which accounted for Denise's revulsion.

It was a voodoo doll, painstakingly detailed to resemble Catalina. And through the mouth of the ghastly symbol was skewered a long, deadly-looking pin!

Chapter Eleven

Shuddering, Denise stepped forward for a closer inspection of the voodoo doll. Whoever had fashioned the horrible thing had done their job with artistic cunning. The hairstyle, the meek expression — down to the last detail it *was* Catalina!

No wonder the girl had taken one look at it and fainted!

More of Amalie's work, Denise thought grimly. But why would the *mambo* have chosen to frighten one of her own followers?

She dashed into the bathroom for a cold, damp cloth to lay across Catalina's forehead. "Come on honey — wake up," she pleaded.

Once again, her gaze fell upon the voodoo doll. She knelt down, trying to disengage it from Catalina's fingers before she revived. But her friend's grasp tightened convulsively, and Denise gave up the struggle, realizing that by tugging she might only succeed in scratching herself or Catalina with the viciously sharp pin.

A door slammed suddenly at the front of the building. Denise jumped to attention. A moment later, hearing cheerful feminine voices, her shoulders drooped in relief. Mama Elena might know how to handle this problem!

She scrambled up, and darted down the hall.

"Please — come quickly," she cried, clutching the housekeeper's plump arm. "Something terrible has happened!"

Mama Elena and the two kitchen assistants who were with her wasted no time on questions. Denise skidded to a halt at the door of Catalina's room, and urged them across the threshold.

"I found her like this," she explained, as the four of them bent over the limp figure on the floor. "Apparently, she came in just ahead of me, and fainted when she saw that — that —"

"Mother of God!" Mama Elena gasped. "What sort of evil monstrosity is this?"

Rosaria's eyes had widened in terror. *"W-Wanga!"* she stuttered. "Black magic! The spell has killed her!"

"Get ahold of yourself. She's only fainted," Denise snapped at the superstitious girl. "Carmen, run and fetch Dr. Baca. Ask him to hurry!"

Carmen seemed only too glad to leave the room. Rosaria's hands were trembling, and she inched backwards toward the door as though she wished that she, too, could flee. No amount of urging could persuade her to approach the voodoo symbol.

By working together, Denise and Mama Elena finally managed to pry the doll loose from Catalina's grip.

"See the way the pin has been jabbed through its mouth?" Denise pointed. "It looks to me as though Catalina is being warned to keep silent. But about what?"

"I do not know," Mama Elena said, darting a nervous glance at the still unconscious girl. "But this is bad — very bad."

Distastefully, Denise dropped the doll into a drawer, out of sight. "At least we needn't look at the nasty thing," she grimaced. "Let's see if we can lift her onto the bed. I wish the doctor would hurry!"

As soon as they had hoisted Catalina into a more comfortable position, she applied another damp cloth to the girl's brow. This time it had the desired effect. A moment or two later, Catalina's eyes fluttered open. She stared blankly at the anxious faces grouped around her.

Denise held her breath, praying that Catalina would not remember the evil object which had given her such a shock.

"Better now?" she smiled.

Catalina's lips parted, but no sound came forth. An expression of sheer terror twisted her face. Her right hand jerked up. She stared at the empty palm, then gazed frantically around the room.

"Be easy," Mama Elena tried to soothe her. "Rest for a little minute. There is nothing here to frighten you."

Once again, Catalina attempted to speak. Incredulously, she raised both hands to cup her throat when for the second time her lips moved soundlessly.

A panicky shriek from Rosaria fractured the stunned silence. In other circumstances, her headlong flight through the door might have seemed comical. Narrowly missing Dr. Baca, she plunged down the hall as fast as her churning feet could propel her. But there was no hint of laughter on the faces of Mama Elena or Denise when they greeted the doctor.

Carmen had graphically described the discovery of the voodoo doll to him, so they were spared that explanation. His countenance, never exactly sunny, turned even more grave when his repeated attempts to coax a word from Catalina proved futile.

He beckoned Denise and Mama Elena over by the door, where they could confer without the patient's overhearing.

"I am going to send her to a hospital," he informed them. "Although there is nothing organically wrong with Miss Ruiz, her vocal chords would appear to be paralyzed." He gestured helplessly. "It is a state of mind, you see. Perhaps a psychiatrist can help her. If not . . ."

"She might never speak again?" Mama Elena whispered in agitation.

Dr. Baca shrugged. "It is quite possible."

"But — but that's like admitting you believe in magic and witchcraft," Denise stuttered. "How could a pin through a doll actually injure someone?"

His solemn gaze told her that she had much to learn. "It can do no harm — unless the victim has absolute faith in the powers of *Wanga*," he said. "I have known cases where strong men sickened and died within a week because they were convinced that a curse had been placed upon them. It is the same with this girl. She *believes* she cannot speak. Therefore, she is unable to utter a word."

"How horrible!" Denise shivered.

She ran back to sit consolingly beside Catalina. "Don't look so afraid," she begged her friend. "Dr. Baca is going to take you to the hospital. No one will be able to harm you there. And — and I'll come see you, just as soon as I can."

Catalina nodded in understanding. But her lovely dark eyes were still shadowed with dread, and Denise sensed that she faced the trip to the hospital with resignation rather than hope.

They had almost finished packing a small suitcase for the girl to take with her when brisk footsteps clattered down the hall.

"Oh, there you are!" Natalie exclaimed, peering in. "What in heaven's name has kept you? Roger has been ready to leave for twenty minutes — he's practically worn his eyes out of their sockets, peering around for you!"

"I *am* sorry. I forgot all about it!" Denise confessed. She hung back indecisively, but it seemed obvious that there was nothing more she could do here.

"All your friends will be thinking of you," she said, giving Catalina's hand a last, reassuring squeeze. "Please take good care of her, doctor."

Natalie was frowning in perplexity when they left the room. "I wish someone would tell me what's going on," she complained.

"I don't exactly know, myself." Denise detoured quickly into her own bedroom, and snatched up the first swimsuit which came to hand. "We'd better go find Roger. I'll explain while we're in the boat."

As they hurried down the short-cut to the beach, the girls glimpsed a group of uniformed men striding purposefully toward the building they had just left. Apparently the police intended to search the employees' quarters as well as the rest of the hotel grounds. This grim reminder of the jewel thefts did nothing to lift Denise's spirits. So many strange things seemed to be happening, all at once!

They found Roger fidgeting impatiently with the oars of an old rowboat. He was almost glowering when the girls jogged across the sand toward him.

"Fine thing!" he fumed. "First the police commandeer the motor launch, and then I have to spend hours waiting for the two of you!"

"Oh, simmer down!" Denise retorted crossly. "Roger, I'm sorry, really. But I seem to keep getting involved in the weirdest affairs. Someone just frightened Catalina Ruiz half to death with a voodoo doll. When she came out of her faint, she had completely lost her voice!"

Roger looked interested, but this did not deter him from pushing the boat off into the water as soon as the girls were seated. Shoving the bag of golf clubs against one of the splintery bulkheads, he snatched up the oars and began propelling the boat in the direction of the island.

Natalie, however, was fascinated by the macabre incident. "You mean the poor kid actually can't speak?" she asked, when Denise had finished describing the way the pin had pierced the doll's mouth. "But that's ridiculous! Nobody believes in that sort of hocus-pocus nowadays!"

"That's what you think," Denise sniffed. "I never told you about the voodoo ceremony I attended a couple of weeks ago, did I? Amalie, the *mambo*, had literally hypnotized those people!"

Roger's mouth dropped open. "You were present at one of the rituals?" he demanded. "I didn't think they allowed strangers to witness the secret rites."

"Nobody knew I was there." Denise tried to laugh, but the effort was not completely successful. Traces of fear still lingered whenever she recalled that dreadful night.

"I wore a scarf over my head," she explained, in answer to Roger's puzzled look. "In the torchlight, with my black hair and suntan, I suppose I could have passed for one of the islanders. Good thing, too, because at the very end I saw a fellow I had met once before — the *mambo*'s son, Orestes. He hates all Americans. If he had recognized me as a friend of John Westcott's, he'd probably have twisted my head off like those poor chickens they sacrificed!"

"Golly!" Admiration tinged Natalie's tone. "I'd never have had the courage to go near that place. Was it awfully spooky?"

Denise remembered the blonde girl's trepidation at riding even in the motor launch, and tried to make her description of the primitive ritual as interesting as possible to keep her friend's mind off their present position. Had Natalie not been so engrossed with the eerie tale, she undoubtedly would have balked at putting to sea in an old rowboat.

"Was it ever!" she answered. "The clearing was set down within a ring of trees, and at first the only sound was the throb of *rada* drums...."

Roger, too, listened attentively. The old injury to his back seemed to be giving him no trouble at the moment, Denise noted thankfully. She decided that his desire for peace and quiet must be very great indeed. Imagine risking aggravation of a chronic back condition with a half-mile pull at the oars!

She had not quite finished the story when he beached the boat on the Isle's beautiful sandy coast. The three of them splashed ashore, and fastened the mooring line to a boulder. Then Roger shouldered his clubs, while the girls carried the picnic basket up to higher ground.

"Well, go on," Roger urged. "What happened after those bloody sacrifices?"

"Please! Not before we eat," Denise demurred.

She had taken a peek inside the bulging basket, and saw that in addition to salad and hard-boiled eggs, it contained a generous supply of cold fried chicken. Better to keep her thoughts away from that ghastly spectacle before it affected her appetite!

The salty sea air added zest to the food, and for a time they concentrated on their lunch.

"That was simply marvelous," Natalie sighed at last, when she had emptied her plate for the second time. She leaned back and closed her eyes. "I hope those policemen have finished searching our rooms by the time we return. They certainly looked determined, didn't they?"

"With good reason," Denise nodded. "The island's economy must depend pretty largely on the tourist business. If vacationers should stop coming here, it could be ruinous!" She rolled lazily over on the blanket. "What's your theory about these jewel robberies, Roger? Do you think they'll catch the thief?"

"Hope so, but I doubt it," he drawled. "After all, even if he hasn't made his getaway yet, he'll have had plenty of time to hide the evidence by now."

Natalie seemed to have fallen asleep. The tranquillity of their surroundings, combined with the boat ride and the large lunch, had made Denise drowsy, too.

"Still, he must have had at least one accomplice," she yawned. "Possibly more. Maybe someone will talk."

Her eyelids fluttered shut — then suddenly popped wide open. Talk! Could that be the reason —

Denise bounced up to a sitting position, thoroughly awakened by the idea which had struck her with such abruptness.

"Talk," she repeated incredulously to herself. "And now Catalina can't. There's got to be a connection!"

"Is that a private debate you're holding, or can anyone join in?" Roger teased.

"Look, when a person has been hypnotized, he — or she — can be made to obey all sorts of orders, isn't that right?" she asked excitedly. "I've just figured out how the thief got into those locked suites so easily. The maid — Catalina — opened the door for him, because she'd been told to while she was still in a trance. And she didn't even realize she was doing anything wrong!"

Roger chuckled. "You do get the wildest notions. I suppose the voodoo doll was sent along to insure that this poor hypnotized girl wouldn't tattle on the cat burglar?"

"I think so." But Denise sounded a trifle less sure. She frowned past him into the rippling surf. "It does make sense, Roger, if you link it up with that voice I heard whispering with Orestes that night at the ceremony. It was terribly familiar. I'm certain it belonged to someone associated with the hotel."

"Good Lord! It's a wonder they didn't cart

you away to the hospital along with Catalina!" Roger shook his head. "Just what were these mysterious whispers you overheard?"

"I caught only a few words," Denise admitted. "Something about danger, and waiting — But the point is, someone at the hotel arranged a secret rendezvous with the *mambo*'s son. And Catalina has ties with both the Caribe Azure and Amalie."

Roger stretched, flexing his back muscles. "Well — in a way, so do you," he pointed out, with a sly chuckle. "From what you've said, that bunch sounds like bad medicine. Why don't you be a sensible girl and stick to your swimming? It's safer than mixing with the occult and risking a black magic spell!"

"Darn! You sound just like John," Denise sighed.

He shrugged, and reached for his bag of clubs. "Do what you like, but don't say we didn't warn you. I'm going to practice my chip shots. Care for a golfing lesson?"

"No, thanks." Denise leaned over to straighten the edge of the blanket where he had been sitting. As she did so, her hand encountered a square brown object half-buried in the sand. It flipped open when she picked it up.

"Wait a minute. You dropped your wallet," she called. She glanced back at it, her attention drawn to the picture of a beautiful dark-haired girl which was displayed in the plastic-coated slot next to his identification card.

"She's very lovely," Denise remarked, handing the wallet back to him. "Haven't I seen an enlargement of that same photo in Senor Lorrimer's office?"

"Probably. Her name was Angelina." He gazed somberly at the picture for a moment before shoving the billfold back into his pocket. "Angelina Lorrimer Gates. His sister, and my wife. She was killed in a car smash two years ago."

Denise caught her breath. It must have been that same accident which had nearly put an end to Roger's career!

"I'm terribly sorry," she murmured.

But the golfer had already turned away and was trudging up the slope. For not the first time, Denise berated herself for her lack of tact. However, she couldn't have been expected to realize what tragic memories the mention of that picture would evoke.

She let a handful of sand sift through her fingers. What a lot of sadness she had been encountering lately! Catalina and Luis, Natalie and Vince — nobody's plans seemed destined for a happy ending.

Maybe Cartuga was just plain unlucky!

Natalie had awakened from her short siesta by the time Denise returned from the bath house where she had changed into her swimsuit. The girls made quick work of clearing away the picnic debris. At monotonously regular intervals, they could hear the smack of Roger's golf club against a ball.

"Going for a swim?" Natalie inquired. "I think I'll hunt around for some tiny seashells. Rosaria was showing me how they can be made into darling necklaces and earrings. Maybe I can make a set myself, in time for Mother's birthday."

"What with all the souvenir jewelry you keep sending them, the Engstromm family must be the envy of everyone in Baltimore," Denise laughed. "Go ahead. I won't stay out too long."

True to her promise, she practiced her backstroke for a few minutes, then waded up onto the beach. She was a little surprised to find that Roger had abandoned his golf, and was already stowing the bag of clubs in the rowboat. As she approached across the sand, she saw him contorting his back muscles, twisting this way and that in an effort to alleviate the twinges of pain.

"Is it bothering you much?" she asked sympathetically. "Perhaps I'd better take the oars on our return trip."

"No, I'll be all right. It's just a little stiff," he insisted. "But I think it's time we started back. Someone might be wondering where we've gone."

Denise agreed. Besides, she found herself suddenly anxious to learn how things were proceeding at the hotel. By now, the police might have uncovered the missing gems!

Natalie joined them, clutching a damp handkerchief bulging with shells. "Might as well get it over with," she grimaced, staring across the expanse of water. "I wish Vince were here to hold my hand!"

"Don't be so silly. You'd think we were embarking on the *Titanic!*" Denise helped Roger push the boat free, then steadied it while her companions tumbled in. When they were seated, she swung in and took up her own perch at the bow.

To all three of them, the return voyage seemed considerably longer than the outbound trip had been. Natalie's nervousness accounted for part of this feeling, but Roger's waning strength was the major cause for their slow progress.

Denise eyed him with growing concern. Each pull at the oars left him noticeably more tired, and he often had to pause for a rest between tugs.

"Let's see if we can't change places," she suggested finally. "We've only about a hundred yards to go. I can easily manage to paddle that short a distance."

Roger wearily raised his head. "Well, if you're sure —"

"Of course I am. Careful, now, when you get up. Natalie, sit still!"

But Denise's shout of warning came a split-second too late. Terrified by the sudden rocking motion, the blonde girl sprang to her feet, upsetting the delicate balance of the boat.

Before either of the others could counteract the dangerous sway, they were all flung violently into the water!

Chapter Twelve

"Help! I'm drowning!"

Natalie's frantic scream pierced Denise's ears the instant she bobbed to the surface. As swiftly as she was able, after the stunning shock of hitting the water, she struck out toward her friend.

The overturned rowboat barred her path, and she was forced to detour around it. Even so, it was only seconds before she pulled abreast of the gasping, wildly thrashing girl.

"Stop it, Nat!" she ordered. "I've got you. Lie back —"

Panic-stricken, Natalie fought away from Denise's encircling arm. For a heart-stopping minute the bedraggled blonde head disappeared beneath the surf. Denise plunged down, grasping desperately at the collar of a blouse, and hauled Natalie's face free of the water.

"Calm down or we'll both drown!"

Natalie's slim body went rigid as a chunk of driftwood, but the authority in Denise's tone at last seemed to make some impression on her.

"That's better. Now relax. You've got to trust me!"

The brief struggle, and the necessity of talking, had shortened Denise's wind. She grabbed the edge of the rowboat with her free hand, and tried to regulate her erratic breathing.

Beside her, Natalie whimpered fearfully. "Roger! Is he —"

Sunlight glinting on a red-brown head reassured the girls. "Over here!" they called.

He splashed up to them, clutching at the boat. "Of all the idiotic stunts!" he sputtered. "My golf clubs —"

Denise shook her head. "I saw them sink. Quit complaining. We're still alive!"

Roger's furious scowl deepened. For a minute, Denise thought he actually meant to dive after his lost property. Then, silently admitting the logic of her statement, he turned his eyes toward shore.

Denise realized that he must be desperately tired. "It isn't far," she encouraged him. "Think you can make it?"

He nodded, saving his breath. Awkwardly but with determination he stroked off toward the white beach. Denise watched his progress for a moment, then turned back to Natalie.

"Don't be afraid. Just lie back and let me tow you. OK?"

Natalie's teeth were chattering so hard she could barely speak. She nodded gamely, though. "I — I'll try."

Fortunately, there was not so much as a puff of wind to stir the waves. At any other time Denise would have found the swim easy, even enjoyable. But with Natalie's deadweight to tow, her progress was necessarily much slower than usual. Beneath her suntan the blonde girl's face was white with terror; Denise dared not relax her grip for an instant for fear that she might again begin choking and floundering.

For minutes which seemed endless she swam on, laboring to hold Natalie's head above water and at the same time straining to keep Roger within view. By the time they had covered half the distance, she knew instinctively that he was in serious trouble. Each flutter of his arms looked weaker. Little by little, the sea was overpowering him!

She stared down at Natalie's frightened little face, then back at Roger. She couldn't help them both. Yet neither was strong enough to reach shore on his own!

Suddenly, her smarting eyes caught sight of what appeared to be a vigorously churning whirlpool slashing toward them. Almost before she had time to identify the strange phenomenon, Jose was in their midst. She had never felt happier to see anyone!

Without one wasted motion, the assistant lifeguard hooked a powerful arm under Roger's chest to support his sagging weight.

"You two all right?" he shouted over to Denise.

"We'll be fine. Go ahead," she called back.

With Roger's life no longer her responsibility, she concentrated single-mindedly on the task of bringing Natalie and herself safely in to shore. Half a dozen anxious sunbathers waded out to assist them the last few yards. The girls tumbled onto dry land, panting for breath.

As soon as she could talk, Denise turned gratefully to Jose. "Thanks, friend. We couldn't have made it without you!"

The muscular young Cartugan lad reddened at her praise. "I did not witness the accident, or I would have come to your aid sooner," he apologized. He gestured at one of the hotel guests. "This lady saw your boat capsize, and gave the alarm. I ran down from the pool as fast as I could."

"Thank heaven for you both," Denise said sincerely, including the woman in her appreciation. She saw that Roger was sprawled out, looking forlorn and utterly exhausted, on somebody's beach towel. "Could you get him back to his room?" she asked Jose. "I think he has had enough exercise for one day!"

One of the male bystanders volunteered to help. Together, he and Jose assisted Roger to his feet and half carried him up the slope toward the men's quarters.

Natalie's wan face showed the strain of her terrifying experience, and she was shivering from the drenching and long exposure. But it was she who struggled up off the sand first, holding out a helping hand to Denise.

"L-let's go change before we catch pneumonia," she said, through trembling, bluish lips. "I'd have to use up a dictionary to thank you properly...."

Denise plodded up the path beside her. "Anything for a friend," she laughed. "Just promise me one thing, Nat. Don't ever stand up in a rowboat again!"

It was still surprisingly early in the day. After soaking in hot baths, and drinking the scalding tea which Mama Elena prepared for them, both girls lay down for well-deserved naps.

Denise awoke shortly before five o'clock, feeling thoroughly rested and with no ill effects except for a stiffness in her right arm. It would be silly to stay in bed any longer, she decided. As she opened the bureau drawer to take out fresh clothing, she noticed that the neat stacks of lingerie were slightly disarranged.

For the first time in hours she remembered the police search. With quickening interest she wondered how they had fared. Perhaps the jewel thief was even now in custody!

She dressed hastily in a flaring cotton frock and brushed her short black hair until it glistened. Then, clipping on earrings and thrusting her feet into dainty high-heeled slippers, she left her room and walked quickly down the hall. Entering the community living room at the front of the building, she heard sounds of a disturbance at the door.

"But it is a rule, Senor," Mama Elena was insisting. "No gentlemen allowed inside!"

"Will you at least take a message to her?" an agitated masculine voice implored. "I have to make sure that she's all right!"

Denise hurried forward, smiling reassuringly at the housekeeper as she squeezed past. "I am; I'm fine. But thanks for worrying," she greeted John. "Now bring me up to date on the news."

"News! Who cares? Knowing you're safe is all I really care about!"

John clasped her in his arms, but released her quickly when he perceived that Mama Elena was chuckling at this display of affection. He took Denise's hand and led her around the corner to a bench where they could talk privately.

"Now, what happened?" he demanded. "I only heard about the accident ten minutes ago when I returned from San Marco. Shouldn't you be in bed?"

Secretly delighted by his concern, Denise glossed over the details of their perilous escapade.

"It was poor Roger who suffered the most," she concluded. "Not only did he have to row all that way, but he lost his golf clubs when the boat capsized. He was absolutely heartbroken when he found they'd sunk!"

"Serves him right for sneaking off with the two prettiest girls on Cartuga," John growled. Ruefully, he looked at his watch. "Feel up to walking over to the office? I have to pick up some reports for my boss. We're still waiting for a break in this blasted jewel robbery case."

Denise groaned in disappointment. "Then the search was in vain? What a shame!"

Martin Lorrimer welcomed her with an emotion that was almost embarrassing. To cut short his praises, Denise emphasized Jose's heroic share in the rescue. She then went on to inquire about Catalina Ruiz, and had just been informed that the girl's condition remained unchanged when the telephone rang.

"For you, John," Senor Lorrimer said. "From the Consulate. You may take the call in Leon's office next door, if you wish."

Denise had moved aside while they exchanged remarks, and found herself staring at the portrait on his oversized desk.

Martin Lorrimer noticed her interest. "My sister, Angelina," he said softly.

She nodded. "Only this morning I learned that she was married to Roger Gates. He still feels her loss very deeply."

"We all do," he sighed. "The most tragic aspect of her death is that we, her own family, caused it."

He turned away, but the motion could not hide the bitterness in his voice.

"My mother and I and my cousin Luana all disapproved strongly of Angelina's choice of a husband. Not aware that they were already secretly married, we assumed that they were eloping. We pursued them down a mountain road in an attempt to halt the wedding."

The memory brought tears to his eyes. "I was at the wheel of the car behind them. I sounded my horn — and when Roger looked back, he lost control of their automobile. It crashed into a tree. My sister died on the way to the hospital."

"How dreadful for you all!" Denise whispered. "After a catastrophe such as that, it's a wonder Roger could bear the idea of returning to Cartuga."

"This I do not understand, either," he admitted. "To be truthful, I had been considering a more prominent golfer for the 'pro' job here at the hotel. But when Roger requested the position shortly before our opening, I could not refuse him. We had not welcomed him into our family — but by marrying Angelina he had become a member of it."

Denise remembered that Vince had spoken of the Latin American peoples' loyalty to even the most distant members of their families. "The cousin you mentioned — is she Luana de Cortez, the movie actress?" she asked.

"Yes, indeed. Although she lives in Hollywood now, Luana still considers Cartuga her real home," the hotel owner said proudly. "No doubt you met her at the opening day ceremonies —"

John Westcott burst excitedly back into the room. To Denise's astonishment, he halted a few feet away from where she was standing, and made her an exaggeratedly humble bow.

"Tell me the truth," he pleaded. "Where do you keep your crystal ball?"

"John, have you suddenly lost your mind? What —"

"Today when I got back to the Consulate, I asked our people to check on Orestes Tigue's past record. Just as a matter of routine," he said. "Remember this morning you kept insisting he had some link with the jewel thief? You wondered about his profession."

"Yes, what about it?" Denise had become infected by his enthusiasm. "Don't tell me he really *is* an apprentice second-story man!"

"Better than that," John gloated. "He spent several years in the United States training to become a lapidarist!"

Martin Lorrimer looked utterly confused. "What is a lapidarist?"

"An expert in the art of cutting precious stones!"

John smiled gleefully at the stunned effect this definition had on his audience. "What's more, Orestes was deported from the States last September. The fancy jewelry shop where he'd been employed suspected that he was using their gems to make copies from a specially synthesized type of glass — and palming them off on the customers as the real thing!"

"Great, galloping seahorses!" Denise could have shouted from sheer exuberance. "That's all the proof you need. Orestes is the last link in the chain!"

She ticked a sequence off on her fingers. "First, Amalie put Catalina into a trance. Later, in response to a post-hypnotic suggestion, Catalina unlocked the doors of certain suites. Our burglar, masquerading as an ordinary hotel guest, strolled in, 'borrowed' a necklace or bracelet long enough to photograph it in living color. He returned the jewelry temporarily, passed the photos on to Orestes, who constructed the duplicates. Then, at an opportune moment, they substituted the phonies for the real gems. It's so simple, it's positively diabolical!"

"I agree," John nodded. "In fact, your whole reconstruction is admirable — except for one tiny fault. The thief wasn't a guest at the hotel."

"But that is impossible!" Martin Lorrimer sputtered. "No stranger —"

"The police just finished a thorough background check on every guest who stayed here long enough to have made all five substitutions. Not one of them has been anywhere near the state of Louisiana for several years. Yet the thefts here and in New Orleans were definitely the work of the same gang."

John shook his head. "I'm sorry, Senor Lorrimer. But I'm very much afraid that the thief is a member of your own staff!"

The hotel owner sank weakly into a chair. "This Orestes — he must be made to name his confederate immediately!"

"We've got to find him first," John said grimly. "The authorities are en route to the voodoo temple now. With luck —"

A thoughtful frown puckered his brow. "We can try to get the information another way. Catalina Ruiz. She may not be able to talk, but there's nothing to prevent her from pointing at a picture!"

"We have photos on file of every member of the staff," Senor Lorrimer said eagerly. "Take them! We must recover the gems, or my hotel's reputation will be ruined!"

Five minutes later John left the office with a thick envelope of photographs under his arm. Denise was forced into a near run to keep up with him.

"Let me go with you to see Catalina," she pleaded. "She's my friend. Maybe I can help."

"Honey, we could be there for hours. The idea mightn't work at all." John gave her a quick hug to soften his refusal. "You've had a strenuous day already. Stay here like a good girl, and I'll be back the minute I learn anything definite."

"That's a promise?" Reluctantly, Denise agreed to do as he asked. "But I'll wait up for you no matter how long it takes. The suspense would keep me from sleeping a wink!"

When the rapid crunch of his footsteps had faded away, she turned in the opposite direction. A lavish sunset had created a magnificent, multicolored panorama on the horizon, but for once Denise was immune to its glories.

What a day this had been! It seemed impossible that so much excitement and activity could have been crammed into a single twenty-four hour period. At about this time yesterday she and John had been dancing at the fiesta, enjoying an existence which was almost carefree. Since then, Fate had stepped in, dealing a succession of shocks and unpleasant surprises to practically everyone she knew.

Life at the Caribe Azure would never be the same again!

The large dining hall was filled almost to capacity by the time she pushed through the door and made her way to her regular table. She sat down beside Natalie, relieved to see that the pinched, white look of the afternoon had faded from her friend's face. The blonde girl was gazing up at Vince with eyes that were frankly worshipful.

Natalie swung joyfully around to Denise. "Guess what? We'll be getting married in June, after all!"

"How wonderful! Congratulations!"

"After what happened today, I intend to have her around where I can keep an eye on her. I told her I didn't care if we had to string tennis racquets for a living," Vince declared, in a tone that was not quite joking.

"What's more, I intend to start taking swimming lessons just as soon as possible," Natalie added. "I don't suppose I'll ever learn to love the water, but that scare today taught me a good lesson. All three of us could have drowned because of my foolishness."

"Personally, I hold Roger to blame," Vince grumbled. "What a time to go out rowing! Not that you missed anything of importance over here. The police didn't find a single piece of evidence."

Denise frowned at her salad. "So I heard. That's rather strange, isn't it? I know there are lots of hiding places, but even so —"

Vince nodded. "Senor Lorrimer told me of the latest theory. If the thief is a member of our staff as your boy friend maintains, it does seem peculiar that the searchers couldn't unearth one tiny clue. They took the entire hotel apart, grounds and all. If the gems had been hidden anyplace on the premises, I'm sure they would have discovered them."

"Let's change the subject. I'm too happy to talk about burglaries right now," Natalie interrupted. "Denise, will you be maid of honor at the wedding? I'll need your moral support to help me make it up the aisle!"

Denise accepted the invitation with pleasure. For the rest of the meal the three of them discussed preparations for the forthcoming marriage. But it was obvious that the engaged couple had eyes only for each other, and as soon as they had finished eating Denise tactfully invented a fictitious errand.

She almost regretted this generous impulse when she stepped outside and looked at her watch. Barely nine o'clock! It would be hours yet before John returned from San Marco. Friends to talk with would have made the time pass more quickly.

However, it was too late now to return to the

dining hall. In hopes of finding company elsewhere, she turned down the arcade which separated the kitchen building from the employees' recreation room.

A pair of public telephone booths was situated at the far end of this little connecting breezeway. As she approached, a man stepped out of one of them. He started to walk rapidly away.

Denise recognized the tilt of his shoulders. "Roger! Wait a minute!"

He halted on the edge of the cement. Denise heard an impatient jingling of coins as he thrust his hands into his pockets.

"I'm surprised to see you up so soon," she remarked. "How are you feeling?"

"Oh, I'm all right — thanks to your friend Jose," he said.

But the pale light filtering out from the open windows gave his face a drawn, faintly haggard appearance, and Denise suspected that his disclaimer was not entirely true. His limp, too, seemed intensified as they moved a few steps closer to the building.

"I'm sorry our day of 'peace and quiet' turned into such a fiasco," she told him. "Particularly since you lost your golf clubs. I've been thinking — it wasn't too far out from shore where the boat capsized. Perhaps a diver could retrieve them before they have a chance to rust."

Roger mulled over the idea for a few seconds. "Thanks for the suggestion, but they're not really worth bothering about," he said. "I'd had them for years. It's time they were retired, especially since I got a new set a few months ago."

"Oh." Denise felt slightly deflated. "You seemed so upset, I thought —"

His head swung sharply around. "Thought what?"

"Nothing, really." She laughed uncomfortably. "Mistaken impression, I guess. At the time, though, it did seem that you were angrier at Natalie because of the sunken clubs than for hurling us all out into the water."

They had reached the recreation room door. Denise tilted it open. When he made no move to follow her inside, she hesitated on the threshold. "Well, goodnight. Take care of your back."

"I'll do that," Roger replied. "Goodnight."

What a strange person he was, she thought, sauntering across to the bookcase. Moody. At times he could be so friendly. Like this morning, when he had insisted that she and Natalie share the trip to the Isle with him. Yet now, just a few hours later, he had acted almost as if she were an impertinent stranger!

Thinking it over, she did not believe she had been mistaken about that scene out in the water. Maybe, as he said, the golf clubs were old and not worth retrieving. But at the time he had been livid with rage at their loss!

It occurred to her that the clubs might have held a special sentimental value for him. Perhaps they had been a gift from Angelina, or something of that sort.

Denise reached out for a mystery story, but the brightly jacketed cover made little impression on her. The thought of Angelina brought Martin Lorrimer's poignant story back to her mind. Why, she wondered again, had Roger elected to return to Cartuga where that tragic episode had taken place? Old wounds did heal, but slowly. Two years ago he must have felt very bitter toward his wife's family. If, in that length of time, he had decided to forgive and forget, he was certainly an unusual human being!

She sat down and resolutely opened the book, reminding herself that his private life was none of her business. But she couldn't help remembering his contemptuous attitude toward Luana de Cortez the day they had all arrived from New Orleans. What had he called her? Luscious Luana, that was it. And he had taken a malicious pleasure in encouraging that bevy of porters and guides to descend on the movie actress like a swarm of buzzing gnats.

Hardly the act of one who had forgotten — or forgiven!

It was a relief to jettison these puzzling thoughts when a group of young people drifted in from the dining hall and invited her to make up a fourth in their bridge game. Denise made a real effort to concentrate on the cards. Nevertheless, her absent-mindedness might have been remarked upon, had not the other three players been less than attentive to the play themselves.

Their conversation revolved largely around

the search the police had made earlier in the day.

"The latest rumor is that they suspect one of *us* of having stolen those silly old jewels," one girl said indignantly. "Can you beat that? Where are we supposed to have hidden them?"

"Nowhere around here, that's for sure," Natalie's assistant, a cute redhead named Jean Barlow, declared. "They spent an hour rummaging through our equipment lockers. As if they expected to find a bracelet or two tangled in a tennis net!"

Denise forgot about the bidding entirely. "They even searched the sports equipment?" she repeated. "Everything?"

"I'll say! Right down to inspecting the racquets for hollow handles. I imagine they looked in the pool, too. Wouldn't it be funny," jean giggled suddenly, "if all that time you had been swimming around on top of a half-million dollars' worth of gems — without even suspecting they were down there?"

Denise's blue eyes widened to the size of saucers. "Jean, you're a genius!" she cried, leaping up from the table. "I'll bet that's just exactly what I *did* do!"

Chapter Thirteen

Heedless of the astonished gasps which greeted this proclamation, Denise dropped her cards on the table. "Excuse me," she apologized to her bridge partners. "There's something I have to see about — right away!"

She was almost running by the time she reached the door. But once through it she forced herself to pause, to reconsider the notion which had struck her with such blinding force.

Was it really possible?

Impetuosity had always been her downfall. Often in the past she had tactlessly blurted out the first thing which came to mind, or leaped to conclusions which were later proven to be completely erroneous. But this was serious. Much too grave a matter to risk making a mistake.

She dared not make an accusation without being absolutely certain that she was right!

Denise paced up and down, fingers laced tightly together behind her back. There could be an alternate explanation. The thief *might* have passed the gems to Orestes for safe-keeping. But she did not believe this was true. *He* was in command, and the snatches of conversation she had overheard that night at the voodoo ceremony gave her the impression that Orestes was a not-quite-trusted accomplice.

Then where else? Cartuga wasn't like the States, where every bank boasted a safe-deposit vault. No, he *must* have kept them close by, in a spot he considered very, very secure. But the thoroughness of the police probe would have uncovered even that most secret hiding place — *if* they had come across it in their search.

And they hadn't. Because when they looked, it wasn't there!

Denise nodded emphatically to herself. The theory, improbable as it seemed, explained everything. Even the motive was crystal-clear now! But would anyone believe her?

The luminous hands of her watch pointed to eleven-fifteen. Too late at night to rouse sleepy police officials, to try, without evidence, to convince them of the necessity for prompt action. She glanced desperately at the phone booths. A bad hour, too, for cutting through hospital red tape. John had doubtless left there ages ago, anyway. By this time he could be en route back to the Caribe Azure.

If only she could count on that!

Yet caution warned that further delay could be costly, even ruinous. Denise bemoaned her earlier thick-headedness. All the clues had been there — but until Jean's remarks tied the strands together, she had completely overlooked them!

Impelled by a mounting sense of urgency, Denise fled toward the main building. Martin Lorrimer's word carried weight. Once convinced, *he* could muster the authorities!

The hotel lobby was practically deserted and the owner's office dark and vacant. As a last resort, Denise scurried around to the reception desk. The drowsy clerk on duty gaped in surprise at her request, then shook his head. She could not speak with Senor Lorrimer, he declared, since both he and Senor Perdigo had departed for San Marco at ten o'clock. There had been a telephone call, a matter of some importance, no doubt. . . .

Sick with disappointment, Denise turned away. Then her shoulders stiffened. She couldn't merely stand by and do nothing. What was needed now was action. And it looked very much as if it were up to her to provide it.

Alone!

That doleful word echoed in her ears as she hastened along the familiar path to the women's quarters. Only a single lamp burned in the lounge, a beacon for late-comers. The workday started early for most of the hotel employees, and she realized that Mama Elena and the other girls must have retired for the night an hour or more ago.

Swiftly, Denise crossed the empty room and continued on tiptoe down the corridor to her own small suite. There she sat down at the writing table and penned a short but concise statement. In it she set forth her theory, naming the thief and the spot where she believed the gems to be hidden, and declaring her intention of attempting to recover them. She inserted the note into an envelope, sealed it, and scrawled Martin Lorrimer's name across the flap. As a further precaution, she slid the envelope beneath Mama Elena's door.

"There!" Denise thought grimly, returning to her own room, and kicking off her shoes. "If anything happens to me, at least they'll know whom to question!"

Two minutes later, clad in a snug, one-piece bathing suit, with rubber-soled shoes on her feet and a blue terrycloth robe swinging from her shoulders, she silently let herself out of the building.

It was a beautiful starlit night. Balmy air touched her skin, as warm as though a few forgotten rays of the sun had lingered to ward off the midnight chill. A whispering breeze curled through the trees, softly ruffling their leaves. A night for music and romance, thought Denise — not skulduggery, or desperate attempts to retrieve a handful of cold, hard stones!

Nevertheless she walked softly, keeping to the verge of the path to eliminate the crunch of gravel underfoot. Intent on her destination, she was oddly reluctant to reach it, and part of her mind urged her to retreat while there was still time. She thrust the temptation aside. The need to tread softly, to descend the curving slope without being seen, kept her concentration riveted on the ground ahead.

It was for this reason that Denise failed to

notice the tall form which approached the lamplit room seconds after she had left it. Had she glanced around, she would have seen him lift his hand to the door, then draw it back. A lazily rolling pebble directed his attention to the path. By the pale illumination of the three-quarter moon he caught a glimpse of her billowing robe vanishing beyond the bend.

Quickly, but just as soundlessly as she had gone, he moved to follow.

The dense tropical foliage thinned, became sparser as Denise continued her descent. Gradually, she became conscious of a new sound added to the rustle of leaves — the hiss of surf hurling itself against the beach, and its sighing retreat into the depths again. When the gravel gave way to sand she began to run, hurrying across the damp, deserted expanse before reluctance overruled determination.

Behind her another pair of feet increased their pace, closing the gap.

Denise flung off her robe, paused to take her bearings. Just here, she thought, on a direct line from the left column of the arch. Only hours ago she had swum toward this point, slowly, wearily, with two lives depending upon her reaching it. She had an excellent eye for distance, for pinpointing a spot where no landmarks showed. One hundred yards out —

The surf frothed in again, and she stepped toward it. A hand caught her wrist, arresting the motion.

"And just where," asked John Westcott sternly, "do you think you are going?"

Denise whirled around, swallowing, a split-second before it erupted, a scream that would have aroused the entire hotel.

"J-J-John! You scared me silly! What are you *doing* down here?"

"Following you, although when I set out I wasn't at all sure of my quarry's identity," he said. "As promised, I returned to tell you the news. But I had just started to rap when I saw someone skulking down the path, and thought I'd better investigate. So here we both are."

"What news?" Denise demanded, staving off the questions which hovered on his lips. "Did you see Catalina? Did she tell you —"

"She showed me," John corrected. "She pointed to a picture. Care to guess whose?"

Denise shook her head. "I don't think I need to. I figured it out — everything. It was Roger Gates, wasn't it?"

John scowled at her. "You knew?" His tone sounded crestfallen, but only for a moment. With the air of a magician pulling a second rabbit out of the hat, he added, "What's more, Amalie Tigue and Esteban Madero have been arrested. Madero left Haiti on a fishing boat and arrived in Cartuga a few days ago. Amalie was hiding him — and Myra Hendricks' necklace, which is now in the hands of the police!"

"How wonderful! Now all we have to do is recover the rest of the jewels before Roger and

Orestes get their hands on them!"

"I have a feeling you're still one step ahead of me," John confessed. "What made you so sure that Roger was the thief?"

"Tonight after dinner Jean Barlow mentioned that the sports equipment had been ransacked by the searchers like everything else in the hotel," Denise told him. "Then she laughed, and said something about the pool — how funny it would be if I'd been swimming around on top of the gems all that time. And all at once the whole thing just fell into place. That's just exactly what I *had* done — only not in the pool!"

She pointed out at the rippling waves. "Out there!"

"I get it!" Suddenly, John snapped his fingers. "In the golf clubs!"

"The only piece of sports equipment the police didn't search — because Roger took them away just before the hunt began," she nodded. "That explains why he was so anxious for us to go on the picnic with him, even at the cost of rowing over. It would look so much more natural if the three of us went together. And since his new clubs were left in the locker room for the police to examine, they'd have no reason to suspect what he had done. No wonder he was so furious when Natalie tipped over the rowboat!"

"All that hard work at the bottom of the sea," John said.

Denise shuddered. "But not for long. I met him coming out of a phone booth earlier tonight.

Unless I miss my guess, he was calling Orestes to come help him fish them out!"

"And you meant to beat them to it? Plucky, but not too smart," John admonished her. "How did you expect to see, once you got down there? And what had you planned to use for air?"

Without waiting for an answer, he helped her on with her robe, then led her back up the slope they had just descended.

"Luckily, all that scuba gear is still in the jeep," he whispered. "But before we do anything else, I want to phone for reinforcements."

Denise waited nervously while he closeted himself in the booth. The recreation room was a dark, vacant shell now, instead of the friendly haven it had appeared an hour earlier, and the entire hotel seemed to be not only asleep, but hibernating. How long, she wondered, would it take the authorities to make the drive out from San Marco?

She was acutely aware of the passage of time during their hike to the parking lot. Actually, no more than ten or fifteen minutes elapsed before they were once again hurrying across the sand, their arms filled with underwater gear, but Denise felt as if the tension had been building for hours.

Perhaps they were already too late!

There was little chance to brood, however, for John had already strapped on his aqualung and was untying one of the skiffs from its moorings.

"Too risky to use the launch," he murmured.

"Let's hope our friends aren't watching the beach through binoculars. Got the flashlight?"

Denise nodded, and clambered into the boat. Even the creak of the oars sounded loud as gunshots to her straining ears. She couldn't resist throwing an anxious glance over her shoulder at the receding coastline. No one leaped forward to intercept them, though, and after a moment she relaxed slightly and concentrated on pinpointing the spot where the rowboat had overturned.

"Funny to think of a top-ranking golfer turning to a life of crime," John mused, while his powerful strokes propelled the skiff out into deeper water.

"Yes and sad, too. He could have become a great champion."

Denise stared at the moonlit waves. "I imagine he met Orestes in Cartuga several years ago, and joined forces with him later on in New Orleans," she surmised. "That dreadful accident must have embittered him terribly."

John remarked that he had learned of Roger's marriage to Angelina only that night. "Senor Lorrimer mentioned the fact that they were related when he and Leon Perdigo drove in to identify the Hendricks woman's necklace," he said.

"Poor Angelina. I should think Roger began plotting his revenge against the Lorrimers while he was recuperating in the hospital. After he and Orestes successfully pulled that diamond robbery in New Orleans, it probably occurred to him that the same plan would work even better at a resort motel catering to a wealthy clientele," Denise speculated. "That way he could ruin the Caribe Azure's reputation, get even with the Lorrimers, and get rich at the same time. He was right, too. The scheme went perfectly until Mrs. Duff tried to dance the limbo!"

"What a scare it must have given him when you spotted that necklace in Haiti!" John chuckled. "Now we know why Madero vanished so quickly. No doubt either Roger or Orestes alerted him that very same night. I suppose that was when they decided to hold on to the rest of the jewelry until it could be safely smuggled into South America!"

Denise squinted back at the shoreline. "This is about the right distance out," she said. "Row a few yards to the left, now. We were on a direct line with the column of that arch."

John jockeyed the boat into position, and let out the small fishing anchor to keep the skiff from drifting away on the current. Before going over the side, he checked both Denise's equipment and his own to make sure that the gauges were working properly.

Down into the depths they plunged, keeping close together. The fragile moonlight penetrated no more than a few feet below the surface. Murky water, merely dim at first, shaded gradually into an enveloping, utterly black cloak of darkness.

The strong beam of John's flashlight pierced

the deep stretches ahead of them. Denise gratefully eyed the glow, aware that without it they would have had no chance at all of accomplishing their mission.

How foolish she had been, to consider making the dive alone!

By night the ocean floor was much colder than the bottom of the lagoon had been, although the depth was no greater. She scrubbed her arms briskly, hopefully encouraging her frostbitten blood to circulate. But physical discomfort was the least of their worries. Had she judged correctly? she wondered. Or were the golf clubs doomed to be lost forever?

John paced out squares with mathematical precision, efficiently eliminating the chance that they would search the same area again and again. Both of them leaped excitedly forward when the glow illuminated a rounded hump ahead of them. Denise could have wept with disappointment when their discovery proved to be nothing more valuable than a rusted, five-gallon can filled with sea water.

Their time was running low, while ahead and to all sides the shifting sands stretched endlessly. It was hopeless, Denise thought despairingly, to keep on. She had missed the site, probably by half a mile —

Her toe nudged something round and hard and smooth. She pounced on it, steeling herself for another failure, but when her hands identified the shape she held it jubilantly against the flashlight's beam.

A pickle jar! The same brand which had accompanied them on that ill-fated picnic — and the label still adhered to the glass!

With this clue to guide him, John hunched low, making a minute search of the immediate area. The light flickered across a litter of crockery, forks, spoons, a pop bottle. . . .

They both saw it at the same instant. Even before the ray had traveled the length of the bag they were stumbling eagerly toward it. The dark, sodden leather moved flaccidly beneath their touch. Denise, grasping the strap, was practically jerked off her feet by its weight. Appalled, she glanced up at John. They would never be able to hoist it to the surface!

John, however, refused to let this difficulty deter him. Kneeling, he reached inside and scooped out the clubs. He placed them in her arms, then laboriously upended the bag. In this position it seemed much more buoyant. Holding it clumsily but with determination, he jerked his thumb upward in command.

The ascent was complicated by their awkward burdens. The handles of the clubs were slippery to the touch, and Denise clutched them with numb, trembling fingers, terrified that they would slip and plunge downward once again. But before they had climbed even halfway to the surface, a new worry beset her. Their oxygen supply was almost completely gone!

Her hearthrob beat loudly in her ears as her lungs labored, straining for air. John's touch spurred her on. Blindly, Denise obeyed. She sucked in the last dregs of oxygen remaining in the tank and held her breath, striving with all her might to reach the surface before being forced to exhale.

Their two heads popped above the waves simultaneously. Denise ripped the useless breathing device away from her face, raggedly drawing in great gulps of air. Gradually, the pounding in her ears abated and the laboring gasps eased.

"Okay now," she panted. "But I nearly suffocated!"

"Me too. My own dumb fault. I forgot to keep an eye on the gauges," John puffed in apology. With a grunt, he hauled the bag onto the rippling wave crests, where it could be more easily handled.

They treaded water for a few minutes, too spent for further exertion. Then Denise pointed to a low, dark shadow gently bobbing ten or fifteen yards distant.

"The S.S. *Queen of Cartuga* awaits. Shall we go aboard?"

John paddled over to the skiff, and with her support wrestled the weighty leather bag over the side. One by one the golf clubs clinked in beside it. Finally, with a great many sloshings that threatened to swamp the boat, he and Denise tumbled onto the now soaking boards.

"I just hope your theory holds water!" he joked.

Denise groaned. "I won't want to hear that word again for at least a week!"

Nevertheless, her spirits had reached a new peak of excitement. While John manned the oars and headed the skiff back in toward shore, she snatched up one of the golf clubs and shook it experimentally.

"It seems solid enough," she frowned.

But after exchanging it for a second iron, her morale shot upward again. "The base of this one feels thicker. And it's much lighter!"

"Probably he carried a couple of genuine clubs, just in case he was forced to use them," John opined. "I wonder if the bag is bogus, too? It weighs enough to be stuffed with gold bullion!"

Denise prodded the squishy leather. "This looks like the same outfit he carried off the plane with him. The Customs inspectors waved us right on through. But I remember he didn't let it out of his sight for a minute, not even while we were in the car. Natalie and I rode with our feet propped up on it, all the way to the hotel!"

Laughing, she glanced across at him. "A diamond-lined footrest! Won't that be something to tell my grandchildren about!"

"Our grandchildren," John firmly corrected her. "You won't mind, will you, if their parents are born in some pretty strange-sounding places? My job is liable to take me to Nairobi or

Tel Aviv or Kyoto. . . ."

Denise could look ahead without misgivings now. Whether African, Jew or Japanese, the people would probably have much in common with the Cartugans — and Americans. It would be fun meeting them, learning their ways —

"So long as it takes me there, too," she smiled. "I won't mind at all!"

In that happy moment she could easily have forgotten about the strange cargo they were carrying. But the coastline was looming nearer every second, and turning to eye the darkened, silent hotel and the tangle of foliage which separated them from it, Denise felt a tingle of apprehension.

"Shouldn't the police be here by now to meet us?"

John, too, stared uneasily ahead at the dense growth. It was thick enough to conceal an army of friends — or foes.

"They should," he agreed. "It will be a relief to hand this contraband over to someone in authority. I don't know how smugglers stand the suspense!"

Denise paused for another searching look at the landscape where the skiff had been tied to a piling. The waning moon shed a mere gloss on trees and shrubbery, without giving any real illumination. Perhaps it would be best to wait — here, in the open. . . .

John, however, was inclined to risk the short, if spooky, climb. "Another five minutes in those wet clothes and you'll be blue all over, to match your eyes," he declared, hoisting the dripping golf bag to his shoulder. He thrust the clubs inside and took her elbow, marching her across the sand.

"Walk now. Worry later!"

Shivering harder, Denise tried, not quite successfully, to obey this advice. Roger and Orestes had lost their desperate gamble, she told herself. By now they had undoubtedly fled the island. . . .

Her squeaking shoes encountered the first patch of gravel. Up the short path — and home!

But just then the foliage stirred. With menacing softness of step, a shadow glided forward. To Denise's terrified imagination, the form looked tall and burly as any tree.

A second dim shape, shorter, stockier, even more familiar, joined the first. Before she could sidestep or even scream, a hand clamped roughly down over her mouth.

"Thanks very much," Roger Gates chuckled nastily, "for saving us all that trouble!"

Chapter Fourteen

Roger's right hand pinioned Denise's arms in a relentless grip, while his left pressed even more ruthlessly across her mouth to prevent an outcry.

"Yes indeed," he continued to gloat. "You've made up nicely for your friend's blunder of this afternoon!"

"Let go of her!" John cried furiously, preparing, if necessary, to use the golf bag as a battering ram. But Orestes stood between him and Roger, and the huge islander lumbered forward to press home his advantage. Hampered by the sodden burden he carried, John was forced back from the path onto the sand.

Denise watched in horror as those massive hands lunged savagely for his throat. Orestes missed his target by mere inches and slowed momentarily when John swung in retaliation, thrusting the heavy leather bag against his attacker's shoulder. But the blow seemed only to increase Orestes' desire for vengeance, for after one staggering step backward he leaped furiously at John again.

In the melee, the wet carrying case was hurled aside, landing with a ringing clatter of clubs several feet from where the men battled. Roger's eyes followed it avariciously, and for an instant his iron grip slackened. Timing her move perfectly, Denise lashed back against his shin with her heel.

The kick landed with a squishy thud. Roger grunted in pain, snatching his hand away from her face and clapping it to his bruised leg. While he was still off balance she twisted violently, wrenching her wrists out of the cumbersome, loose-fitting robe. Even as she jerked free she screamed, a high, piercing shriek which vibrated loudly through the still night air.

Before the last echoes of the cry had faded away she was sprinting across the sand, ready to come to John's aid if a way could be found to do so. The two combatants were still locked in their deadly bout. Fighting for his life — and hers — John kept jabbing short, swift punches at the aggressor, while dodging to evade the hammering force of Orestes' powerful fists.

She darted a glance over her shoulder, just in time to see Roger scuttling across to where the golf bag lay abandoned. Relief flowed over her for the space of one ragged breath. At least he was making no effort to recapture her!

Suddenly, though, relief changed to horror. With surprising agility and speed the golfer swooped down and plucked a club from the sheath. Moonlight glinted on the slim, strong shaft, and outlined the wicked steel base of the weapon as he swung it high overhead.

Like a cat preparing to pounce, Roger crept nearer the battlers. Denise realized that he was only waiting to strike until his opponent should seem most vulnerable. In another moment, the iron would come crashing down on John's skull!

Desperately she reversed her course, scooping up a handful of sand as she raced to avert that disastrous blow. Just as the club began its downward sweep, she flung the damp, gritty particles straight at Roger's face!

The direct hit blinded him momentarily. With a yelp of rage he stumbled away from the other men, dropping his weapon and tripping over another of the protruding clubs. Even before his stinging eyes were able to focus he was clawing at the sand, making frenzied motions to stuff the irons back inside the bag.

Denise eyed him warily, trying to anticipate his next move. Not until he had staggered up, with the bag of clubs clasped tightly in his arms, did it dawn on her that he was running out on the fight — and taking the loot with him!

Ten feet behind her, a savage blow thudded home. Denise whipped around, biting her lip in anguish as blood spurted from a cut in John's forehead. Somehow, she had to help him! He couldn't dodge and weave much longer. Another solid hit such as that last one, and the battle would be lost!

"Orestes!" she screamed frantically. "Roger is running away with the jewels! He's deserting you!"

As she had prayed, her cry diverted the young giant's attention for a vital half-second. His head jerked around, and angry black eyes lighted on his absconding partner. But at that precise instant, John's fist rocketed against his jaw! Orestes toppled to the sand, his outraged bellow ending in a groan.

Swaying unsteadily, John stared down at his fallen opponent. A look of utter astonishment spread over his face, and his bruised lips attempted a grin in Denise's direction.

"Saved by the bell," he muttered. "Count him out, will you, honey?"

With that, he collapsed wearily alongside Orestes!

"John! Oh, you poor darling!"

Intent on trying to revive him without disturbing his sparring partner, Denise missed seeing the half-dozen flashlight beams which bounced and flickered across the landscape and then converged at the top of the slope. The sighing surf and feeble moans of the fallen gladiators also kept more commonplace noises from reaching her ears.

But to those waiting at the head of the path, the crunch of gravel disturbed by a limp was a sound which loomed all-important. Men froze into position and lights winked abruptly out as Roger, puffing laboriously, emerged from the cover of trees and trudged around the bend.

He was still seething with rage, and he resolved that at some future date Denise would pay for the injury and humiliation he had suffered. Now, however, his main concern was to escape while Orestes still fought on to cover his retreat. Time enough to plan revenge when he and his new fortune were safely aboard a jet bound for Buenos Aires!

At last the fatiguing climb was over. The encroaching foliage, trees and bushes, fell away from the path — to be replaced by strangely animate shadows, all of which were closing in on him! Police whistles shrilled imperiously, and the precious bag was jerked from his grasp.

Handcuffs snapped across his wrists. Meanwhile other officers, quickly descending, took charge of a bruised and battered islander, and two very wet, very tired young people who seemed to have been out for a moonlight swim!

Denise smiled across the table at John. This Tuesday luncheon in San Marco was their first opportunity for a private chat in quite some time, but very few ideas had been exchanged. They had spent most of the past hour gazing into each other's eyes.

"Can you believe that all the commotion is over at last?" she asked.

Gingerly, John touched the bandage which concealed a sizeable portion of his forehead. "Over, but not forgotten. This lump is a pretty tangible reminder," he grimaced. "Still, it could have been worse. And at least people have stopped asking us questions!"

The day and one-half just previous to their reunion had been a hectic time for them both.

On Sunday night, or rather the small hours of Monday morning, a brief explanation to the police had sufficed, but the following day their testimony was required by a half dozen interested authorities. John and Denise had completed detailed official statements until their writing hands ached.

Naturally, the story had to be told and retold to friends and acquaintances as well, and a new flurry of excitement rocked the Caribe Azure when it was disclosed that the missing gems had been recovered. Denise suspected that all the publicity had only served to enhance the hotel's popularity, since reservations continued to pour in, even for the hot summer months ahead.

"In a way, these thefts might prove to have been a blessing in disguise," she mused aloud. "The newspapers are emphasizing the part voodoo played in the crimes. The people aren't likely to remain devoted to a *mambo* who has confessed to hypnotizing and hoaxing her own followers!"

John nodded in agreement, remarking how different Catalina had seemed that morning from the mute, frightened girl he had interviewed Sunday night.

"Learning that Amalie was in jail must have shattered the spell," he chuckled. "I guess she realized that if black magic couldn't keep the *mambo* out of the hoosegow, it couldn't really hex anyone, either. That fellow Luis seemed mighty pleased when Catalina started talking again."

Denise smiled at the remembrance. "Didn't he, though? I have an idea wedding bells will be chiming out all over Cartuga in the next few months."

"So long as there's rice enough left over for ours!" Scooting a little closer, John twined his fingers around hers.

"Actually," he added, "I feel rather sorry for Senor Lorrimer. Here he went to the trouble of hiring three well-known athletes for his sports crew, and what happens? Both girls decide to get married, while his golfing 'pro' turns out to be practically the master criminal of the year!"

There was a look of laughter in his grey eyes. Gazing up at the man she loved so dearly, Denise chimed in with a merry chuckle.

"I guess that in that field, Roger really *was* a champion. Nothing but the best for the Caribe Azure!"

The employees of G.K. Hall hope you have enjoyed this Large Print book. All our Large Print titles are designed for easy reading, and all our books are made to last. Other G.K. Hall books are available at your library, through selected bookstores, or directly from us.

For information about titles, please call:

(800) 223-1244
(800) 223-6121
To share your comments, please write:

Publisher
G.K. Hall & Co.
P.O. Box 159
Thorndike, ME 04986